The Gingerbread Girls

Coming together in time for Christmas

The Gingerbread Inn was where best friends Emily, Andrea and Casey spent much of their childhood. Now all grown up, they're back—older, wiser, but still with as much need for a little Massachusetts magic than ever. As Christmas approaches and three gorgeous men appear on the scene, is it time to create some new treasured memories?

Don't miss

The Christmas Baby Surprise

by Shirley Jump in October 2013

Marry Me under the Mistletoe

by Rebecca Winters in November 2013

Snowflakes and Silver Linings

by Cara Colter in December 2013

Dear Reader,

Happy holidays! I absolutely love the holiday season and all the fun, family and food that it brings with it (especially the food!). Second best to celebrating the holidays is writing a holiday continuity with other authors. We had a lot of fun planning the Gingerbread Girls series and writing about the fabulous Gingerbread Inn.

This book is all about second chances. Cole and Emily's marriage is in shambles, and when Emily escapes to the inn that she loves, the last thing she expects is to have Cole show up and ask her for a second chance. The older I get, the more I understand and appreciate the importance of redemption, forgiveness and second chances for all of us. That's what made this book such a joy to write.

So pour a mug of tea, curl up somewhere warm and take a trip to the Gingerbread Inn, where happy endings are just around the corner.

Happy reading,

Shirley

The Christmas Baby Surprise

Shirley Jump

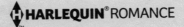

Recycling programs
for this product may
not exist in your area.

ISBN-13: 978-0-373-74263-9

THE CHRISTMAS BABY SURPRISE

First North American Publication 2013

Printed in U.S.A.

HARLEQUIN®
www.Harlequin.com

New York Times bestselling author **Shirley Jump** didn't have the willpower to diet, nor the talent to master under-eye concealer, so she bowed out of a career in television and opted instead for a career where she could be paid to eat at her desk—writing. At first, seeking revenge on her children for their grocery store tantrums, she sold embarrassing essays about them to anthologies. However, it wasn't enough to feed her growing addiction to writing funny. So she turned to the world of romance novels, where messes are (usually) cleaned up before The End. In the worlds Shirley gets to create and control, the children listen to their parents, the husbands always remember holidays, and the housework is magically done by elves. Though she's thrilled to see her books in stores around the world, Shirley mostly writes because it gives her an excuse to avoid cleaning the toilets and helps feed her shoe habit.

To learn more, visit her website at www.shirleyjump.com.

Books by Shirley Jump

THE MATCHMAKER'S HAPPY ENDING
BOARDROOM BRIDE AND GROOM
MISTLETOE KISSES WITH THE BILLIONAIRE
RETURN OF THE LAST McKENNA
HOW THE PLAYBOY GOT SERIOUS
ONE DAY TO FIND A HUSBAND
FAMILY CHRISTMAS IN RIVERBEND
THE PRINCESS TEST
HOW TO LASSO A COWBOY

Other titles by Shirley Jump available in ebook format.

To my husband,
who makes everything better with his smile.

CHAPTER ONE

WHEN EMILY WATSON ran away from her life, she did it in style. A pair of dark brown skinny jeans, four-inch heels, a shimmery cream shell, all topped with an oversize green cardigan belted at the waist. The clothes were designer, the shoes custom-made, but Emily didn't care. The labels had never mattered to her, and a part of her missed the days when she bought jeans at the Goodwill and topped them with a ratty T that had been washed until the cotton became soft as silk.

She threw a couple suitcases into the trunk of the Volvo she'd bought, even though Cole had hated the big boxy car, then drove away from the house that no longer felt like home. Four hours later, she wound through the hilly roads of Brownsville, Massachusetts, then past glimmering Barrow Lake, until the big leafy trees parted, exposing the long gravel road that led up to the Gingerbread Inn. A small hand-painted sign with a wooden arrow pointing up the hill announced the inn, the familiar marker faded by time.

She rolled down the window and took in a deep breath of fresh, sweet fall air, along with the sense of being home. At peace. Finally.

The tires of Emily's Volvo crunched over the gravel, sending pebbles scattering to the side. Anticipation filled her as she made her way up the road. Finally, she was back here. In the one place where life made sense, the one place where she had found peace, and most of all, the one place where she hoped to find herself again.

She put a hand over her belly. Too soon to feel anything more than an almost-imperceptible curve beneath her pants but Emily had taken to talking to Sweet Pea, as she'd dubbed the baby inside her. "Almost there, Sweet Pea."

And there, Emily vowed, she would start a new life. She'd left almost all remnants of her old life behind, to come here and get some time to think, plan, strategize her next move. Because no matter what, Emily Watson refused to return to the status quo. Or return to Cole, the man she had once loved. The man she had married—and now was ready to divorce.

Once upon a time was a long, long time ago. The years spent in a lonely, unfulfilling marriage had taught Emily that fairy tales should be reserved for the foolish.

The two-story Georgian-style inn came into view. Shaded at first by the late-fall sun above, it looked sad, lonely, dark. As she drew closer, Emily slowed the car. The anticipation built, then as her eyes adjusted and she saw the full view of the inn, her anticipation imploded into disappointment. What had happened?

The once white gingerbread trim had faded to a dingy gray. Paint peeled off the wooden clapboards, and the wraparound front porch sagged in the center, as if the inn was frowning. Weeds sprang up among the stones of the walkway, and the landscaping that had once been so beautiful it had been featured in a local gardening magazine had become overgrown and tired.

But that wasn't what hit Emily the hardest. It was the red-and-white For Sale sign tacked to the building, hanging a little askew, as if even the Realtor had lost hope.

She parked, got out, but didn't take a step. What was she supposed to do now? She'd counted on staying at the Gingerbread Inn, not just for an escape, but as a way to find closure and connection. A long time ago, she had formed her best memories here, with Andrea and Casey and Melissa—

Oh, Melissa.

Just the thought of her late friend made Emily's heart ache. But Melissa had made it clear she wouldn't want that. *Get on with your life and your dreams,* she'd written in her final letter. *Don't let anything hold you back.*

Don't let anything—even a For Sale sign?

Emily's hand went to her belly again. She had to do this. Not just for herself, but for Pea, too. Sure, she could afford to stay at a hotel, even jet to Italy and spend a week in a villa, but that wasn't where Emily's heart lay. It wasn't the place she needed so desperately to be right now.

Emily glanced down at her hand, at the ornate diamond ring in its platinum setting. She slid it off and tucked it in her pocket. It was time to accept that she was moving on.

Away from Cole.

The front door of the inn opened, and a petite gray-haired woman came out onto the porch. She had on a deep orange apron with yellow edging, a pale pink T-shirt, a pair of denim shorts and sneakers that had seen better days. Emily's face broke into a grin, and she crossed the drive in fast strides. "Carol!"

The inn owner's face lit with recognition and she came hurrying down the steps. "Emily Watson? Oh my goodness, I can't believe it's you!"

The two women embraced, a long hearty hug, the kind that came from years of friendship. Emily had spent so much time at the inn in the summers of her childhood that Carol seemed more like an aunt or an extra grandmother than the owner. She still carried the scent of home-baked bread, as if everything good about the world surrounded Carol Parsons.

A wet nose nudged at Emily's jeans. She grinned and looked down at a golden shaggy dog that had a little Golden in her, a little something else. "Is this Wesley's daughter?"

Carol nodded. "Meet Harper. She's a bit of a mutt, but she's lovable and goofy and all the things you want in a dog."

Emily bent down and ruffled Harper's ears. "You've got a heck of a reputation to live up to, missy."

The dog wagged her tail, lolled her tongue and looked about as unworried as a retriever mix could look. Then she turned and bounded off into the woods, barking an invitation to play at a squirrel.

Emily rose. "I'm so glad you're still here, Carol. When I saw the For Sale sign, I was afraid…"

"Don't you worry. I'm still here. Hanging on by a thread, but here. Anyway, that's a sad story for another day." Carol gestured toward the inn. "Do you want to come in? Stay a while?"

"Actually…" Emily pointed toward the bag in the back of her car. "I was hoping to stay a long while."

Carol's green eyes searched Emily's, and then her face filled with compassion, understanding. "You stay as long as you want, dear. There's always a room for you here."

That was what Emily loved about Carol. She'd never asked questions, never pried. Merely offered a helping hand and a shoulder to cry on, whenever one was needed. Emily hadn't had that kind of bond with her own mother, or heck, any of the female relatives in her family. But she had with Carol, and had looked forward to her summers here as much as she looked forward to sunshine after a cloudy day. She'd spent more time in the kitchen of the inn, helping Carol knead bread and peel potatoes, than probably anywhere else in the world.

The two of them headed inside the inn. The porch creaked a warning as Emily crossed the rotting floorboards. The swing needed a coat of paint, and several of the balustrades had fallen to the ground below. The front door still had the large beveled glass panel that defined its elegance, but inside, everything else looked old, tired, worn. The hardwood floor of the foyer had darkened with age, and one of the parlor's windows rattled against the breeze trying to make its way under the sill. A water stain on the ceiling spoke of plumbing trouble above, while the steam radiators hissed and sputtered a weak wave of heat to break fall's chill.

Emily stowed her bag by the door, then followed Carol into the kitchen. This room, too, had been hit hard by time. The once-bright and happy sunflower wallpaper was peeling, and the white vinyl floor was scuffed and torn in some places. The same long maple table dominated the center of the kitchen, flanked by eight chairs, enough for the help to have dinner, or a few up-too-late teenage girls to grab a midnight snack.

Carol crossed to the coffeepot. "Do you want a cup? I've also got some bread that just came out of the oven. It's warm, if you want a slice."

"No coffee, but I'd love some bread. Who can turn down that bit of heaven? Do you have honey for it?"

"I do indeed. If there's one thing that's still producing here, it's the bees." Carol grinned, but Emily could see the pain behind the façade. Carol retrieved two mugs of coffee, a plate of bread slices and some honey before returning to the table. She held her cup between her hands and let out a long sigh. "I bet you're wondering why this place looks like this and why I have it up for sale."

"Yeah, but I understand if you don't want to talk about it." Emily had plenty going wrong in her own life that she wasn't keen to discuss, either.

"It's okay. It's been hardest for me to tell the regular guests. Those people are like my family, and to think that the Gingerbread Inn will one day no longer exist…it just breaks my heart. But there's only so much I can do." Carol dropped her gaze to her coffee. "After my husband died, this place got to be too much for one person. Revenue dropped off when the economy struggled, and I just couldn't afford to hire people to keep up with the maintenance. I love it here, I really do, but it's got to the point now where the whole thing is too much. I don't even know where to begin to repair and rebuild. So I put it on the market. Maybe I'll get enough money to pay for a little cottage near the beach."

Harper wriggled through the dog door in the kitchen, took one look at the two women and ducked under the kitchen table, her tail beating a comforting patter against the tile floor. Carol gave the dog a loving pat.

"I hate to see you sell it. I like knowing the inn is here, if…" Emily sighed. "If I ever need it."

Carol's green eyes met Emily's, and her face filled with concern. She reached out, covered one of Emily's hands with her own. "What's the matter, honey?"

"Just a lot going on in my life right now," Emily said. An understatement if there ever was one.

This morning, she'd walked out on her ten-year marriage. They'd already been separated for six months, but separated was a loose term when it came to Cole. He'd stopped by at least once a week, for everything from his favorite golf club to checking to make sure the lawn mower had enough gas for when the landscapers came by.

It was as if he didn't want to accept it was over. Okay, she hadn't made that message any clearer by sleeping with him again. One crazy night, fueled by nostalgia and memories, and she'd forgotten all the reasons they were wrong for each other. The reasons she had asked for a separation. The reasons why she couldn't live with a man who broke her heart almost every day.

Emily finally realized that if she wanted space, she'd have to get it for herself. And with the new life inside her, she needed to have a clear head to make one big decision.

File for divorce or try one more time.

"Well, you take whatever time you need," Carol said. "If there's one thing this place is perfect for, it's thinking."

"I'm counting on that," Emily said, then got to her feet for a second slice of bread. It didn't help her think, but it sure helped her feel like she'd come to the right place. Something about being back at the Gingerbread Inn filled her soul, and right now, Emily Watson needed that more than anything.

* * *

Cole Watson bounded up the stairs of his house—okay, technically it wasn't his right now, even if he was still making the mortgage payments—with a bottle of wine in one hand and a dozen roses in the other. He reached for the front door handle, then paused.

This was Emily's house now. That meant no barging in, something she'd made clear more than once. He lived in a condo across town. A space of his own that was as empty as a cavern, and still echoed loneliness when he walked in at the end of the day. *That* was his home, like it or not, and this place no longer was, which meant he had to stop acting like he could barge in, grab the remote and prop his feet on the coffee table. He rang the bell, even though it felt weirder than hell to ring the bell of a house he still wrote a check for every month. Waited. No answer. Rang it again.

Nothing.

He fished out his key—she'd never changed the locks, something he had taken as a good sign—unlocked the door and went inside, pausing in the vast two-story foyer. Even fully furnished, professionally decorated, the massive house felt empty, sad. Seven thousand square feet of gleaming marble and granite, and it seemed…

Forlorn.

The same copper bowl he remembered them buying on a trip to Mexico sat on the foyer table, waiting for his keys. A neat stack of mail addressed to Cole sat beside the bowl under the Tiffany lamp he had bought for their first anniversary. In the parlor to the right, the same white love seat and armchairs that Emily had hated and he had bought anyway sat, facing the east garden. And down the hall, he could see the wrought-iron kitchen table and chairs, a gift from his mother years ago.

The house was the same, but…different. Off, somehow.

Then Cole spied the slip of paper atop the mail and realized why. He laid the wine and roses on the foyer table and picked up the note.

Went out of town. Don't know when I'll be back. Don't call me. I need some time to think. To figure out my next step.
Emily

The cold, stark words hit him hard. They were separated. Did he think she was going to leave him some gushy love note? Still, the reality stung, and reminded him that the marriage he thought he had and the one he did have were two very different things.

Went out of town. Where? Why? With someone?

That thought pained him the most, and drove home the other fact that Cole had yet to face. If he and Emily couldn't repair their marriage, then at some point she would move on, find someone else. Another man would see her smile, make her laugh, hold her in the dark of night.

And rightly so, because they were over and had been for a long time. Didn't matter if Cole was having trouble accepting the fact.

Against his hip, his cell phone buzzed. He flipped it out and answered the call. "Cole here."

"We've got a wrinkle in the product launch," said Doug, his project manager. "There was a bad storm in Japan, and the plant that's supposed to make the screens for us was damaged pretty heavily. They aren't sure when they'll be back online."

"Call someone else."

"I did. There's a backlog on the materials. Seems we wiped out the inventory. It'll be two weeks before they can produce more—"

"I'll take care of it. Get me on the first flight to…" Cole fingered the note in his hands. *I need some time to think. To figure out my next step.*

The next step. There were only two options—get back together or get divorced. It didn't take a rocket scientist to figure out which way Emily was leaning.

Don't call me.

She didn't want him to contact her. The bridge he'd hoped might still be there between them, the connection he'd been counting on when he'd shown up with wine and roses, was gone. She'd underlined the words. Made it clear she didn't want him coming close.

His marriage was over.

"Cole? Did you want a flight to the plant in Japan? Or to the manufacturer in Poland?"

Cole Watson, who had never had an indecisive moment in his life, stood in the empty foyer of the house he no longer lived in and wavered. "Uh…"

He glanced at the note again. *Figure out the next step.*

Then he glanced at his left hand. At the gold band that still sat there, and had for the past ten years. He imagined it gone, imagined this house gone, sold. Neither of those thoughts gave him more than a flicker of loss.

But then he glanced at the five letters at the bottom of the note. *Emily.*

Gone.

That thought ripped a seam in his heart. He crumpled the note in his fist and dropped it into the copper bowl. It circled the bowl, then landed with a soft plunk in the center. "The screens can wait," he said to Doug. "I have another matter to take care of first."

"But, but—"

"Don't worry, Doug. I'll handle it." Cole could hear the panic rising in Doug's voice. The man had a tendency to panic first, think second. "By the time I'm through, we'll look back at this moment as a blip on the radar. A momentary setback."

But as Cole hung up the phone and tried to figure out where in the world his wife might have gone and how he was going to deal with whatever next step was coming his way, he realized he wasn't talking about the screens at all. He was talking about his marriage.

CHAPTER TWO

IN THE SMALL but cozy bedroom where she'd spent many a childhood summer, a blank computer screen and blinking cursor stared back at Emily, waiting for her to fill it with words. Something it had been doing for the past twenty minutes. She'd type a word, backspace, delete. Type another. Backspace, delete. What had happened to her? In college, she had been able to write short stories like a chicken producing eggs. Now when she finally had time and space to write, she couldn't manage to get a word onto the page. This was her dream, and all she could do was stare at it.

Her focus had deserted her. Heck, it had left town months ago. She needed to get her priorities in line again. Somehow.

A light fall breeze whispered through the couple inches of open window, dancing with the white lace curtains and casting sparkles of sunshine on the white-and-blue space. The low sounds of a radio playing downstairs, probably while Carol worked, made for a harmony with the chatter of the birds outside. It was a serene, perfect setting, the kind of place any writer would love to have. Well, any writer without writer's block, that was.

Emily crossed to her bag, and tugged out the envelope she'd tucked into the front pocket. Melissa's last note, mailed to her, and she presumed, also to the other girls.

Dear Gingerbread Girls,

I'm laughing as I write that little nickname for us. Remember those crazy summers we had at the Gingerbread Inn? All those adventures in town and late at night? It's no wonder someone dubbed us the Gingerbread Girls. Heck, we were always together, thick as thieves, Carol used to say.

I miss that. I know we've all got older and have gone on with our lives, but oh how I miss those summers, those connections. That's the one big regret I have now. That we couldn't figure out a time for a reunion and now it's too late. I won't get to see you all one last time.

Promise me you'll get together. Promise me you'll keep the Gingerbread Girls alive. Promise me you'll all follow your dreams, the ones we talked about that day by the lake. I still have my rock. Sometimes I hold it and think back to that day.

You are all the best friends I could ever hope for and I will be forever grateful for the summers we spent together.
Melissa

Tears blurred the letter in Emily's eyes. She drew in a shaky breath, then propped the letter beside the computer, holding it in place with a small oval stone that she had kept with her for the past fifteen years. Somewhere out there, two other matching stones sat in drawers or on desks, or somewhere. Did Andrea and Casey see the stones the same way? Did they remember that day?

The women had fallen out of touch over the years, separated by busy lives and families. Maybe it was time to get the Gingerbread Girls back together. Before Emily could think twice, she shot off a quick email to both Andrea and Casey, including her cell phone number and an invitation to come to the inn. She left off the news about the For Sale sign, because she hoped to find a way to talk Carol out of that choice.

And in the process, she would write this book, damn it. She would follow her dreams. Emily needed this do over. Needed it…a lot.

A knock sounded on the door. Emily got to her feet and opened the bedroom door to Carol. "Good timing," Emily said with a laugh. "I've got writer's block on the first word."

"I've got some coffee and cookies that should help with that," Carol said. "But first, there's someone here to see you."

"Someone here to see me?" How could that be? She'd told no one where she was going, and had only sent the email to the other girls a couple minutes ago. Unless they were in the driveway when they got it, there was no way either Andrea or Casey could show up that fast. No one else would be able to track her down so quickly. No one but—

"Cole."

Carol grinned. "How'd you guess? Yes, he's here. Waiting in the parlor to talk to you." Then her good friend's face fell. "Are you okay, honey? Do you want me to tell him to come back later?"

"No." Emily knew Cole and knew he wouldn't take no for an answer. The qualities that had made him a successful business-man had made him a terrible husband. Win at all costs. That pretty much summed up Cole. When they'd been dating, she'd seen that atti-tude as one that meant he wanted her and their life together more than anything in the world. But she'd been wrong. What Cole wanted, more than anything or anyone, was success, regardless of the cost to attain it. Then as the years went on, he'd employed that approach to arguments, major decisions, everything. She'd had enough and walked away.

But Cole refused to get the message.

"I'll talk to him," Emily said. "Just give me a minute."

"Sure, hon. Take whatever time you need. I'll talk his ear off. Might as well make him suffer." Carol let out a little laugh, then put an understanding hand on Emily's arm. "If it helps, he looks miserable."

Emily thanked Carol, then shut the door. She faced her reflection in the oval mirror that hung over the antique dresser. She was still clad in a pair of pale blue flannel pajamas, her hair in a messy topknot on her head, and her face bare of makeup. She looked a million miles away from Cole Watson's wife.

Perfect.

Without doing so much as tucking a wayward strand of hair back into place, Emily spun on her sock-clad feet and headed out of the room and down to the parlor. She no longer cared what she looked like when she saw Cole. She was no longer going to be the woman who stressed about every crease, every spot, who worried about her public image as the CEO's wife. She was going to be who she was—before.

Cole stood by the window, his back to her. He wore a tailored dark blue suit that emphasized his broad shoulders, tapered waist, the hours he spent in the gym. His dark hair was getting a little long and now brushed against the back of his collar. Her heart skipped a beat when she saw him, just as it always had. That was one thing that had never changed—her attraction to him. Her hormones had never listened to her brain.

He turned as she approached, even though she'd made almost no sound entering the room. "What are you doing here?" he said, or rather, barked.

So much for some kind of tender moment. What had she expected, really? They were no longer together, and maybe someday her heart would get the message. "How did you find me?"

"There is only one place in the world that you have talked about missing, and it's this place. I took a chance that's where you'd go, and I was right."

Well, he'd listened to her talk about the inn. Too bad he hadn't listened to any of the other problems between them. "Where I am and what I'm doing is no longer your concern, Cole," she said.

"You're my wife, Emily."

"We've been separated for six months. I'm not your anything anymore."

His face took on a pained look, but it disappeared a split second later. "Be that as it may, I should at least know where you are, in case something happens."

"Well, now you know." She turned on her heel and headed out of the room.

He caught up to her, his hand reaching for her, but not connecting, as if he'd just remembered they were no longer together. She noticed the glint of gold, the ring he still wore. Because he hadn't thought to take it off? Or because he hadn't given up yet?

"Wait," he said. "Don't go. I want to talk to you."

She wheeled around. When she met his blue eyes, a little hitch caught in her throat. A hitch she cursed. "We're done talking, Cole. Nothing's changed in ten years—nothing's changing now. Just—" she let out a long sigh "—let me go. Please."

And this time, he did just as she asked. Emily walked out of the room, and Cole didn't follow. She paused at the top of the stairs, waiting until she heard the click of the door. Then she returned to her room, put a hand on her belly and told herself she'd done the right thing.

Cole stood on the ramshackle porch for a long time. How had it got to this point? What had he missed?

There had been a time when he could smile at Emily, or take her out for a night on the town, and whatever was wrong between them would disappear for a while. But this time, he'd sensed a distance, a wall that had never been there before. Or maybe he'd just never noticed it until now.

Until his wife had crossed two states to get away from him. To this place, this...inn.

He glanced at the run-down house behind him. The overgrown grounds. The peeling paint. Why had Emily come here, of all the places in the world? With what they had in their joint bank account, she could have afforded a five-star hotel in the south of France. Instead, she came to this…

Mess.

Frustration built inside him, but there was nowhere to go with that feeling. Nowhere but back home to New York, and to work. He took a step off the porch, and as he did, a crunch sounded beneath his foot and the top step crumpled beneath his weight, sending his leg crashing through a hole and down onto the soft earth below. He let out a curse, then yanked his leg out.

The door opened. Cole's hopes rose, then sank, when he saw the inn's owner, Carol, not Emily, come onto the porch. "Are you okay? I thought I heard a crash," Carol said.

"The step broke." Cole put up a hand of caution. "That porch isn't safe. You might want to block it off or hire someone to fix it."

"Okay." One word, spoken on a sigh, topped by a frown.

Cole had been in business long enough to read the signs of a beleaguered owner, one who had more bills than cash. "I could call someone for you. Considering I broke the step, I should be the one to fix it." Sympathy filled him. He still remembered those early, cash-strapped days when he'd been building his business, watching every dime and trying to do everything himself. Sacrifice had been at the top of his to-do list for many years.

Carol shook her head. "I couldn't possibly ask you—"

"Consider it done," Cole said. He had his phone halfway to his ear before he reconsidered.

Fixing that board would only take a minute or two. Calling someone to fix that board would take a lot longer. At least an hour, even if he paid a rush fee, to get someone out here, just to nail a board in place. Judging by the looks of the place, the inn's owner had enough problems on her plate without adding in a wait on a contractor.

"If you have some nails and a piece of wood, I could put in a temporary fix," Cole said. Where the heck had that come from? He hadn't done contractor work for years. His hands were so soft from working at a desk they might as well be mittens.

"I have lots of supplies," Carol said, pointing to a building a few yards away. "Help yourself."

"Will do." Maybe it would feel good to work with his hands again. And maybe he was just trying to delay leaving, hoping for a miracle with Emily.

Carol went back inside, so Cole headed for the garage. It took him a little while, but he found a tape measure, some plywood and a hammer and nails. He measured the space, ripped the board on a dusty table saw, then hammered the wood onto the risers. The actions came naturally to him, as if he had never walked away from construction.

The sun beat down on him, brought sweat to his brow and a warmth to his back. He had hung his suit jacket over the porch rail, taken off his tie and rolled up his sleeves. By the time he finished, all four stairs had new treads. And yes, it had probably taken as long as it would have taken had he called someone, but he had the bonus of feeling like he'd done something productive. Something he could look at and see, an almost-instant result, the opposite of how things happened when he made decisions at his desk.

Emily came out onto the porch. Surprise lit her features when she saw him. "What are you doing?"

"Fixing the board I broke. Then I noticed the other steps were about ready to break, so I replaced those, too."

She moved closer and peered over the railing at his work. "You still remember how to do all that?"

"Like riding a bike." Cole leaned against the handrail, which he'd made more secure with a few nails earlier. "It was just like the old days."

Did she remember those days? That tiny apartment they'd lived in, how they'd rushed home at the end of the day, exhausted but excited to see each other? She'd bandaged his cuts, he'd bring her a glass of cheap wine, and they would sit on the fire escape and watch the city go by. The world would be perfect for a little while.

"I guess you don't forget some things," she said.

"No, you don't." But he wasn't talking about hammers or measurements or anything related to construction. "Do you remember those days, Em?"

"Of course." Her voice was soft, her green eyes tender, then she cleared her throat and drew herself up. "We've moved a long way away from those days, though. In more ways than one."

He pushed off from the rail and stood beneath her. "What if we could get them back?

What if we could be the people we used to be? Would we have a chance then?"

She bit her lip and shook her head. "Fixing some steps doesn't bring us back there, Cole. You've changed…I've changed. What we want has changed. You can't turn back the clock." She gave the railing a tap. "Have a safe trip back."

Then she went inside and shut the door, closing the door on him, as well. Cole stood there a long, long time, then picked up the tools, returned them to the garage, got in his car and drove away. He'd done all he could here, he realized. And the sooner he accepted that fact, the better.

But as he left the Gingerbread Inn, and the run-down building got smaller and smaller in his rearview mirror, Cole wondered…if he could turn back the clock with the inn, maybe it would be enough to turn back the clock with his wife, too.

CHAPTER THREE

By BREAKFAST THE next day, Emily had ten pages written and a swelling sense of satisfaction. They might not be good pages, heck, they might not even be publishable pages, but they were closer than she'd got to her dream of publishing a novel in years. All those years in high school and college when she'd written short stories, and made fits and starts at different novels, but never finished any of them. Now with hours of uninterrupted time, her creativity exploded, with pages springing to life as fast as she could write them. She got to her feet, stretching after the long hours in the hard wooden desk chair.

Nausea rolled through her in a wave. She gripped the back of the chair, drew in a deep breath and waited for it to pass. It didn't.

"Hey, kiddo," she said to her belly, "I thought this was supposed to end with the first trimester."

The baby, of course, didn't answer, and the nausea kept on pitching and rolling her stomach, neither caring that the calendar said Emily was just past three months pregnant. Her clothes still fit, if a little snugly, but she knew it wouldn't be long before she would start to show.

And that would mean telling people about the baby. People like Cole.

Emily sighed. She loved her husband—she really did—but she had stopped being *in* love with him a long time ago. She'd tried, Lord knew she'd tried, to make it work, thinking maybe if she kept acting like a wife, she'd feel like one. But the relationship they had had when they'd first got married had drained away, like a hose with a pinhole. The loss had come so gradually that one day she'd woken up and realized it was over, in her heart, in her head, and continuing the facade would only hurt both of them. Six months ago, she'd asked Cole to move out, and he'd gone, without a fight.

Then Cole had come to her one night, telling her he'd do anything to have his wife back. He'd been so sincere, so racked with sorrow, she'd believed him, and found the old passion ignited. One crazy night, a night where she'd believed yes, he finally got it, and maybe they could make it work—

And in the morning he was gone, off on yet another business trip. She was left alone again. She'd had a good cry, called a lawyer and filed for a formal separation.

Two weeks later, she'd realized her period was late and that one night had resulted in the only thing Emily had ever wanted—and Cole never had.

A child.

She'd kept the pregnancy a secret, and kept her distance from Cole, resolving to do this on her own. Now she had a baby on the way into her life and a husband on his way out. Either way, Emily was determined to make her new existence work.

She pulled on some sweatpants and an old T-shirt, then headed out of her room and downstairs toward the kitchen. A little dry toast should take the edge off this nausea, and then she could go back to work on the book.

Emily was just reaching for the loaf of bread on the counter when she heard a *tap-tap-tapping* coming from outside the window. She leaned over the sink, and peeked out into the bright late-fall day.

Cole stood on a ladder, perched against the

side of the building, hammering in a new piece of siding. He'd switched from dress clothes to a crisp new pair of jeans and a dark blue T-shirt that hugged the planes of his chest. Sunglasses obscured his blue eyes, and a leather tool belt hung at a sexy angle from his hips. For a second, her heart melted.

"He was here when I woke up this morning," Carol said as she entered the kitchen.

Emily turned around and put her back to the window. What did Cole think he was doing? Did he think that fixing the inn's porch would fix them, too? "Why?"

"I don't know. I'm just glad for the help. Anything he can fix helps me in selling this place."

Emily sighed. "It's going to be so weird not to have this place here anymore. The Gingerbread Inn is such a big part of my childhood."

Carol paused by the coffeepot. "Do you want a cup?"

"Uh, no. I'll have tea instead." Emily grabbed the kettle off the stove, filled it with water, then set it over the flame. Outside, Cole had stopped hammering. Emily resisted the urge to look outside and see what he was doing now. Maybe if she ignored him, he'd leave. Either way, he rarely stayed away from the office for more than a few hours, so whatever "fixing" he was doing would be done soon and Cole would go back to being his usual Type A, nose-to-the-grindstone self. She'd be on her own, just her and the baby, which was exactly what she wanted, she told herself. Her hand strayed to her stomach, a protective barrier.

Emily looked up and noticed Carol watching her. "What?"

"Tea, huh?"

Emily fished an herbal tea bag out of the glass mason jar next to the stove and held it up. "Yup."

"Decaf, too. In the morning." Carol cupped her hands around her mug of coffee and assessed Emily. "Anything you want to share?"

"Nope, nope." She'd said that too fast, Emily realized. But she wasn't ready to tell anyone about the baby yet. She thumbed toward her room. "I should get back to writing. I'm on a roll."

If she stayed in this kitchen one more minute, she was sure Carol would read the truth in her face. The kettle whistled and Emily turned to pour the water. She heard a sound behind her and pivoted back.

Cole stood in the kitchen, watching her. In jeans and a T-shirt, he looked so much like the man she'd fallen in love with that Emily's heart stuttered, and she had to remind herself to breathe. Cole still had the same lean physique as he'd had in college, and her mind flashed images of every muscle, every plane. Her hormones kept overriding her common sense.

Carol murmured some excuse about needing to start laundry and headed out of the room. Emily shifted her gaze away from Cole and down to her teacup. She dipped the bag up and down, up and down, avoiding Cole's blue eyes. "What are you doing here?" she asked him.

"Helping Carol out."

"I can see that." She let out a frustrated gust. "Why?"

"She's obviously in a tight spot right now and—"

"Cole, stop making up excuses for being here. I've been married to you for ten years, and you have never so much as hung a picture in all that time. So don't tell me you got this sudden urge to become Homer Handyman."

"Homer Handyman?" She could hear the smile in his voice, as he crossed the room and poured himself a cup of coffee. "I'm not making up excuses, Emily. I saw Carol needed help, and I wanted to do what I could. I haven't worked with my hands since college, and I have to admit, it feels good."

"Then go home and build a box or something. Don't stay here."

Cole paused in front of her and waited until she lifted her gaze to his. "Home isn't home for me anymore."

She refused to feel bad about that. Refused to let the echoes in his voice affect her. Their marriage had disintegrated, and Cole knew that as well as she did. "Why are you really here, Cole?"

His blue eyes softened, and for a moment, she saw the Cole she used to know. The Cole she had fallen in love with on a bright spring day on the NYU campus. "Because this place means a lot to you," he said quietly.

The cold wall between her heart and his began to defrost, and Emily found herself starting to reach for Cole, for the man she used to know, used to love. Then his cell phone rang, the familiar trill that signaled a call from the company's CFO, and Cole stepped back, unclipping the phone with one hand and putting up a finger asking her to wait a minute with the other.

Emily shook her head, then grabbed her tea

and walked out of the kitchen before she was once again foolish enough to believe that anything had changed.

Chaos had descended on the offices of Watson Technology Development, if the number of calls, texts and emails Cole had received in the past hour were any indication. He'd been gone less than forty-eight hours and people were in a panic.

Rightly so, he supposed, considering he spent more hours at WTD than anywhere else in the world. Ever since the day he'd started it, Cole had dedicated most of his waking hours to the company that bore his name. In the beginning, the hours had been a necessity, as he worked his way up from a one-man office to a global company with offices in three U.S. cities and two foreign locations, building computers, cell phones and custom technology solutions for his customers.

It took him a good hour to calm down his assistant, and to wade through all the crises that needed his attention. The urge to run back to the office and handle everything himself ran strong in Cole, but every time he glanced at the pile of wood and tools, he remembered that he was here for another reason.

Not to fix the Gingerbread Inn—though that was the reason he'd given Emily—but to fix his marriage. Deep in his heart, Cole knew he had run out of chances, and if he let Emily go this time, what they had between them would die like a plant stuck in a dark corner for too long. That was partly his fault, he knew, and the only way to fix it was to stay here. Put in the time, handle the project of his marriage like he did any project at work—lots of man-hours.

When he hung up with the office, he flipped out his phone and made a quick list of everything that the Gingerbread Inn needed done to make it sellable. By the time he got to number fifty, he knew he needed two things—a couple of professionals, because some of the jobs were out of his realm—and a second set of hands.

Another half hour on the phone and he had a plumber, electrician and a roofer lined up to come out and give him estimates. The last call he made was to the one man he knew who would drop everything at a moment's notice and travel anywhere in the world, just because a friend asked him to.

"Joe," Cole said when the call connected.

"How would you like to vacation in Massachusetts for the holidays?"

Joe laughed. "Did I just hear the great and busy Oz say the word *vacation?*"

"It won't be a long one, but yes, I'm taking some time off. I'm working on a project here and could use an extra set of hands." Cole explained about the inn and its owner's financial struggles. "Plus, Em's here."

"She is? How's that going?"

"Not so well. I'm just trying—" he sighed, pressed a finger to his temple "—to give us one more chance. I'm hoping that she sees my being here as being committed to her, to us."

"I always thought you two were going to live a long and happy life together," Joe said.

"Yeah, me too." Cole sighed again.

His friend thought for a second. "Give me a couple days to tie up the loose ends I have here, and then I'll join you. It'll be good to catch up. How long has it been?"

"Too long," Cole said. "Far too long."

He hung up with Joe, then put his phone away and surveyed the work ahead of him. There was plenty to do, for sure. His gaze wandered to the second-floor bedroom where Emily was staying. The room was only twenty feet or so away, but it might as well have been on the moon.

Earlier, in the kitchen, there'd been a moment, a split second, really, where he'd thought maybe he could see a bridge back to them. Somehow, he needed to build more of those moments. One on top of another, and the bridge would connect them again. He hoped.

He headed back into the house and found Emily in the kitchen, opening a package of saltines. She'd changed into a pair of jeans and a fitted T-shirt. The clothes outlined her hourglass shape, the narrow valley of her waist, the tight curve of her rear end, and sent a roar of desire through him. Damn, he'd missed her. In a hundred different ways.

"Hey, Emily," he said.

She turned around, a saltine in her hand. "Cole."

There was no emotion in that syllable, nothing that he could read and pinpoint as a clue to how she felt about him. He cleared his throat, took a step closer.

"I was thinking of taking a break for lunch," he said. "Would you like to go into town with me? I need to get some supplies, too."

"Sorry, no. I'm, uh, working on something."

"Working on something? What?"

"Something personal," she said, and turned toward the cabinet to get a glass.

The door had shut between them, and she had no intentions of opening it—that much was clear. Cole should cut his losses, go back to New York and bury himself in work. Accept the divorce and move on, like she had.

Then why did he stay in the kitchen like a lovelorn teenager? He grabbed a glass of water that he didn't want, hoping Emily would talk to him. Instead, she gathered her crackers and her drink and headed for the hall. "Em?"

She turned back. "Yeah?"

"Is there any chance?"

The question hung in the sunny kitchen for a long moment. Emily's green eyes met his, and for a second, hope leaped in his chest. She shook her head and lowered her gaze. "No, Cole, there isn't."

Then she brushed by him and out of the room, leaving Cole more alone than he could ever remember feeling.

CHAPTER FOUR

Two FRIENDLY, HAPPY emails greeted Emily when she got back to her room. Andrea and Casey, both thrilled to hear from her and chock-full of their own news. Casey, the more dramatic of the three, was full of boisterous stories about her life, while Andrea talked about working at her family shop during tough economic times. They were both surprised to hear the inn was up for sale, and both said they'd try to make it out there before the holidays. "I'd love to give the place one more goodbye," Casey wrote, "and give you a great big hug, too. It'll be great to see you all and maybe raise a toast to Melissa. We'll stand out on the dock and give her a proper goodbye."

Emily wrote back, telling them that sounded like a fabulous idea, and encouraging her friends to arrive as soon as possible. Her hands hovered over the keyboard while she debated how much to tell them. "Things are going great with me," she said finally, lying through her fingers. "Can't wait to see you!" She left it on a bright, cheery note, even adding a smiley face. Then she hit Send, and tried to work on her book again.

The words wouldn't come. After eating the saltines, her nausea had passed, and her stomach rumbled, reminding her it was lunchtime. A lunch she could have enjoyed with Cole, if she'd taken him up on his offer.

Doing so would only tempt her all over again, and the last thing she needed was to be tempted by Cole. She placed a hand on her belly and splayed her fingers against the tiny life deep inside her. "We'll be okay, Sweet Pea. I promise."

Carol poked her head into Emily's room. "I made a salad for lunch. Want some?" Carol noted Emily's hesitation, and added, "Cole left. Said he had to go to town."

"Lunch sounds good. I was just starting to get hungry." Emily shut the laptop's lid, then followed Carol to the kitchen. Harper lay on the small rug in front of the back door, snarfling and twitching, probably chasing a rabbit in her doggy dreams.

Carol laid two heaping plates of spinach,

strawberry and feta salad on the table. Sprinkles of roasted pecans and a raspberry vinaigrette finished off the tasty lunch. "So," Carol said when she sat across from Emily, "when are you due?"

"When...what?" Heat rushed to Emily's cheeks. "What are you talking about?"

"Honey, I may not be able to know how to save this place, but I know when a woman is expecting. The tea, the nausea, the saltines. Plus you just have that look about you."

"What look?"

"That excited-slash-terrified look." Carol grinned. "My sister had three kids, and she looked like that every time."

Emily picked at the salad. "May 17."

Carol's face exploded in a smile, and she jerked out of the chair to gather Emily in a tight, warm hug. "I'm so happy for you, honey."

"Thank you," Emily said, and for the first time, the joy of what was coming began to infuse her. Sharing the news made it real, somehow, and that allowed her to imagine the future with the child she had always wanted.

A child Cole hadn't wanted.

But that didn't matter. She and Cole were over, even if he had yet to fully get the message. She was going to have this baby alone and be just fine. She'd wanted a baby almost from the day they got married. Cole had kept telling her they should wait. For what, she wasn't even sure now. All she knew was that he found one excuse after another not to have a child.

Finally, Emily was building the family she'd dreamed of. Granted, a family without a father, but Emily had no doubt she'd more than make up for Cole's absence.

"Cole must be over the moon about the baby," Carol said.

Emily shook her head. "He doesn't know. And I'm not telling him," she added before Carol said anything. "We've been separated for some time now, and after I get back to New York, I think…no, I know, I'm going to file for divorce."

"What? But then…why is he here?"

"Because Cole is the kind of man who never loses. Even when the battle isn't his to win." She shrugged, and cursed the tears that rushed to her eyes. "Our marriage has been over for a long time, but he won't accept that."

Carol's hand covered Emily's. "I don't know about over, if you have that little gift growing inside you right now."

"That night was a mistake." Emily shook

her head. "One I won't repeat. My marriage is *over*, Carol. I'm just looking ahead to the future with just me and the baby."

The doorbell sounded a happy little trill. "We can talk later," Carol said. "Let me get the door. You stay, finish your salad. And don't worry, I won't say anything to Cole."

Emily smiled up at her old friend. "Thank you."

A minute later, Carol was back with a tall, trim, white-haired man beside her. "I'm not quite sure what all we need done around here," she said as she walked into the room. "My home repair skills are pretty limited."

"Seems to me like you need a little of everything." The man's gaze swept the kitchen, taking in the water stains on the ceiling, the dripping faucet, the worn countertops. "The house has good bones, though, and that's what matters. You've got a great place here, miss."

A shy smile curved across Carol's face. "Oh, I'm far from a miss these days."

The man gave her a grin that crinkled the corners of his pale blue eyes. "I disagree."

Carol let out a little laugh. "Well, thank you, Martin."

They were flirting, Emily realized. Something she had never seen Carol do before.

Carol tore her gaze away from the man and waved toward Emily. "This is Emily, an old friend and one of the regular visitors to the Gingerbread Inn," she said. "Emily, this is Martin Johnson. Cole hired him to do some work around here."

Emily stood, shook Martin's hand. Harper sat in the corner of the kitchen, her tail wagging, while she watched the exchange between the humans with curiosity in her brown eyes.

"I'm mainly a plumber, but I know how to do just about anything. That's what comes from buying my own fixer-upper twenty years ago." He grinned. "I'm still working on it two decades later. The carpenter's always the one who doesn't get time to build his own furniture."

"I bet that drives your wife crazy," Carol said.

"Would if I had one," Martin said. "But my Sarah passed away, going on ten years now."

"I'm so sorry," Carol said. "Listen, we were just having lunch. Could I get you something to eat, and we can talk about the repairs? I've got leftover meat loaf in the fridge if you want a meat loaf sandwich."

Martin's grin widened. "I haven't had one of those for years and years. But I hate to put you out. I'm sure you're busy."

Carol giggled. Actually giggled. "Oh, it's no trouble at all. You sit, and I'll fix the sandwich."

Emily had finished her salad and rose to put her plate in the sink. "Nice to meet you, Martin," she said to the handyman, then turned to Carol. "I'm going to go back to work for a little bit."

"Okay," Carol said. "Be sure to get out and enjoy this bright sunshine, too. It's an absolutely gorgeous fall day."

Emily glanced out the window. "You know, that sounds like a great idea. I think I'll take a notebook and head down to the dock."

"Sounds like a perfect way to spend an afternoon," Carol said.

Martin and Carol started talking about the repairs needed at the inn. Their conversation flowed easily, with a little undercurrent of interest on both sides.

A few minutes later, Emily threw on a thick sweatshirt, then grabbed a notebook and a pen and headed outside. Cole's rental car was nowhere to be seen. A part of her hoped he'd done what he always did—hired someone to do what needed to be done so he could go back to work. Whenever she had something on the honey-do list, Cole would pick up the phone and solve the problem. There were times when she wanted to yell at him that she didn't want hired help. She wanted her husband to be the one to hang the pictures, move the sofa, trim the old maple tree in the backyard. Because that meant he would be home for more than a few minutes, and she'd feel like they were in this life together, not two trains running on parallel tracks that slowly diverged in opposite directions.

The lake's water glistened under the bright sun, as if diamonds had been sprinkled across the smooth, lightly rippled surface. The same wooden bench she remembered sat at the end of the dock, weathered and gray. She sat down, drew her feet up to her chest and leaned against the armrest. The sun warmed her face and shoulders, and soon Emily was immersed in her ideas. She scribbled all over the notepad, plot twists and character details flowing as fast as her pen could put the words on the page.

It was as if a waterfall had been held back too long, she realized. Maybe that's what it was—all those years of trying to be Cole's wife, putting everything she wanted to do to the side so that she could keep the perfect house and the perfect life, then be the perfect wife at banquets and dinners and parties. Her self had disappeared somewhere among the gossip-filled brunches with the other wives, the afternoons spent playing another round of golf while Cole networked. She'd forgotten the ambitions she'd had when she graduated, the dreams she was going to pursue. But now here, finally, she was doing it. Taking Melissa's advice and living her life before it was too late.

"Enjoying the day?"

Cole's voice jerked her to attention. Her pen skittered across the page. "You scared me."

"Sorry. You were so lost in what you were doing there, I guess you didn't hear me clomping down the dock."

"You never clomp, Cole." She chuckled. "You're a little too refined for that."

"Oh, are you saying I've gotten soft in my days behind a desk?"

The word *soft* made her glance over at his trim body, still muscular and strong, thanks to frequent gym workouts. He'd put a thick black leather jacket over the T-shirt and jeans, giving him an almost…dangerous air. The day she'd met him, he'd been wearing a leather jacket much like this one. In an instant, she was back in time, standing on a sidewalk and apologizing for running into Cole because she'd had her nose buried in a book, reading while she'd walked to class. He'd told her she should never apologize for a good story, and as he helped her pick up her schoolbooks, they'd started talking, and it felt like they hadn't stopped talking for a solid month. By the holiday break, she was in love with him and by the end of the school year, Cole had proposed. All because she'd seen the leather jacket and thought he was sexy, and she'd been intrigued by a man who looked like a biker but talked like a scholar.

What was she doing? Getting distracted by the man she no longer wanted?

"Mind if I share the seat?" he asked. "Grab a little break?"

"Sure." She turned, put her feet on the dock and moved to make room on the bench for him. As soon as she did, she regretted the decision. The bench was small, and Cole was so close, it would only take a breath of movement for her thigh to be touching his.

"I got you something when I was in town," he said, and handed her a small brown bag.

"What's this?"

He waved at the bag. "Open it and see."

She peeked inside the bag. A shiny wrapper

with a familiar logo winked back at her. "You got me my favorite snack cakes?"

"Thought you might be craving them."

For a second, she thought he knew she was pregnant, and she panicked. Then Cole chuckled. "If I remember right, you were always craving those things. I think we cleaned out the campus cafeteria on a weekly basis. What'd you use to say?" He leaned back, thinking. "There's always a reason—"

"To celebrate with cake." She took the package out of the bag. "Of course, that's what I said when I had the metabolism of a twenty-year-old."

Cole reached up, as if he was going to brush away the bangs on her forehead, but withdrew without touching her. She swallowed the bitter taste of disappointment. "You're still as beautiful now as the day I met you, Emily."

She got to her feet. "Cole—"

He reached for her hand. When Cole touched her, electricity sizzled in Emily's veins, and her heart caught. "I'm not saying anything other than that you're beautiful, Emily. No reason to run."

It did look ridiculous to hurry off the dock just because Cole had complimented her. She retook her seat. "Let's just keep this friendly, okay?"

"Sure." If he was disappointed, he didn't show it. He propped his feet on the railing in front of him, leaned back on the bench and tilted his face to the sun, eyes closed.

It was as if all the years of stress and long hours melted away. Cole looked younger, happier, more peaceful than she had seen him in a long time. Maybe working on the inn was doing him some good. For years, she'd worried about him having a heart attack at work because he worked too much, ate at odd hours and had more stress on his shoulders than anyone she knew.

"I met Martin," she said, unwrapping the snack cake and taking a bite. It was heaven on her palate. "Did you hire him to do all the work around here?"

"Nope. Just to help on the things I'm not good at. I figure I'll stay a few more days." He opened his eyes and turned to look at her. "If that's okay with you."

How could she say no? He was helping Carol, and Carol desperately needed help if she was going to keep the inn running. Plus, Cole looked so relaxed, so happy, something Emily had rarely seen in him.

When the baby was born, she and Cole would have to be civil. Attend family gatherings together sometimes, or maybe just meet to talk about their child. With the baby, Emily knew Cole would never be totally out of her life. Someday, maybe she'd stop reacting when he smiled at her or touched her. Maybe.

"It's fine, Cole. I'm just surprised you want to do it."

"Working with my hands has made me feel…useful." He chuckled. "I know, I know, they need me at work and that should do the same, but this is different. When I fixed those steps, I saw an immediate response to a problem. One minute they were a hazard, the next they were ready for visitors. It's like every corner of this place is crying out for attention."

She wanted to say that she had done that for years, and he'd never noticed. Or listened. "Maybe we should have bought a fixer-upper instead of built a house. Then you could have had projects all the time."

"You still have that honey-do list, don't you?"

She shook her head. "I gave it to Bob. The contractor you hired to do the renovations on the kitchen? He's taking care of all those things while I'm gone."

"Oh, that's good." He sounded disappointed.

A part of her wanted to believe that if she went back to New York right now, Cole would take up that honey-do list and insist on being home more often, being there, being with her. But the sensible part of her knew this time at the inn was a temporary reprieve. The problems in their marriage ran deeper than a remodeling project. Instead, it would be better, and smarter, to use this time together as a way to forge their future together. Their real future, not a fantasy one.

"Cole..." She paused, laying her hands in her lap, her appetite for the snack cake gone. "I think we should sell the house. I don't need one that big, and you aren't living there anymore and..."

"Let's wait," he said. "Give it some time—"

"We've been separated six months, and really, a divorce is just a formality at this point. The sooner we get these things settled, the faster we can move on."

"What if I don't want to move on?"

The pain in his voice hurt her. She had no doubt he still cared, but she knew how this would end. She'd read this same story a hundred times over the course of their marriage. "Cole, we've tried this. The big fight, the talk of ending it. You come back, try for a few days, then before you know it, you're back at work and I'm in a marriage of one person. Let's just make it official, okay? Instead of pretending that we're ever going to be a family."

She gathered her things and got to her feet. She started to pass by him, when Cole reached out. "Emily."

His voice was harsh, jagged, filled with need and regret. Feelings she knew well because she'd felt them herself. She hesitated, standing on the dock under the bright November sun while the water lapped gently at the pilings, and looked down at the man she had pledged to love forever.

"I'm sorry, Cole. I really am," she said softly, then placed a kiss on his cheek.

At the last second, Cole turned, and his mouth met hers. Heat exploded in that kiss, and Cole jerked to his feet, hauled her to his chest and tangled his hands in her hair. Her mind went blank, and her body turned on, and everything inside her melted. All the perfect little arguments she had against being with Cole disappeared and for a moment, Emily Watson was swept back into the very fairy tale she had thought stopped existing.

CHAPTER FIVE

FOR ONE LONG sweet moment, Cole's life was perfect. Then Emily broke away from him, and stumbled back a step. "We...we can't do that. We're getting divorced, Cole."

He scowled. "I know what's going on between us."

"Then let's stop getting wrapped up in something that's never going to work. We made that mistake a few months ago, and—"

"And what?"

She shook her head and backed up another step. "And it was a mistake."

"So you're giving up, just like that?"

Her gaze softened, and though Cole wished he read love in that look, what he really saw was sympathy. "No, Cole, I never gave up. You did that for both of us a long time ago. And now you're doing what you always do. Fighting to win, because Cole Watson never loses at anything. Too bad you never realized that you lost me a long, long time ago."

He stood on the dock for a long time, listening to the soft patter of her feet as she headed up the dock and toward the inn. The water winked back in the sunlight, bright and cheery. For the hundredth time, Cole wondered what the hell he was doing here and why he was trying so hard to save his marriage when his wife didn't want him to.

The lake blurred in front of him, and his mind drifted back over a decade into the past. To a beach in Florida, a run-down motel and the happiest five days of his life. Things had been simpler then, he realized, before the company and the money and the big house, and all the things he thought would improve their life. Instead, it had cost him all he held dear.

Somehow, he needed to get back to that simple life, to the world that had once seemed to consist of just him and Emily. Then his phone started buzzing against his hip, and he knew doing that was going to be harder than he'd thought.

Emily buried herself in words for two hours that afternoon. She cracked the window, letting some of the crisp, fresh air filter past the lacy curtains and into the room. The sounds of chirping birds and the occasional whine of the table saw broke the quiet of the day. The pages flew by, as she took her characters and had them battle past the challenges in their lives, striving for success, even against impossible odds. The book was going very, very well and each new chapter she started gave Emily a little burst of energy and satisfaction. She was doing it. Finally.

She sat back in the chair and stretched. If only solving her own life problems was as easy as solving those of her fictional characters.

It didn't help that she had complicated things herself by kissing Cole. It was as if there were two parts to her heart—the part that remembered the distance, the fights, the cold war of the past few years, and the part that remembered only the heady beginning of their relationship. The laughter, the happiness and the sex.

Okay, yes, being touched by Cole was the one part of their marriage that had never suffered. Their sex life, when they'd had one, had been phenomenal. He knew her body, knew it well, and had been a wonderful lover.

When he had been there to love her at all.

That was the real problem in their marriage.

Cole's absences, fueled by his dogged dedication to the business, meant he was never home. In the early years, she'd supported him, encouraged him to work as much as he needed, but as success began to mount and Emily thought he would finally cut back on his hours, Cole instead worked more, dedicating weekends and vacations to this new project or that customer problem. He'd poured his heart and soul into the company, leaving almost nothing of either one for their marriage.

She got to her feet, gathering her dishes from her afternoon snack and headed down to the kitchen. Carol was peeling potatoes at the table, and had a basket of fresh green beans waiting to be cleaned beside her. Emily put her dishes in the sink, then sat in the opposite chair and started twisting off the stringy ends and breaking the green beans in half, then adding them to a waiting colander. "I remember doing this when I was a little girl," Emily said.

Carol smiled. "You always did like helping me in the kitchen. Half the time I'd have to kick you out and remind you that you were on vacation, not part of the KP crew."

Emily shrugged. "I liked being here."

"Instead of with your own family."

"We weren't much of a family to begin with," Emily said. "My mother was always off doing her thing, my father was always working. And when they were together, they fought like cats and dogs."

An understatement. Emily's parents' marriage had been mostly a marriage of convenience, two high school friends who'd married at the end of senior year, then had a child in quick succession, before realizing they were better friends than lovers. They had lived separate lives and only came together for birthdays and major holidays. The annual "family" summer vacation to the Gingerbread Inn was more of an opportunity to spend time with their friends and play shuffleboard than to bond as a family. The only time all three of them were together was Friday nights, when they all went into town for dinner at their favorite diner.

Carol picked up a fork and pricked holes in the scrubbed potatoes. "So when you grew up you did the opposite, right?"

Emily let out a little laugh and thought about how she had described her parents. She'd done the same thing, though not on purpose. For years, Emily had done her own thing and Cole had worked. The only saving grace—

they hadn't caught a child in the middle of that mess. Not until now. Emily covered her belly with her palm. When Sweet Pea arrived, she vowed to give her baby the childhood Emily had never had. "I pretty much carbon copied their life. At least I'm smart enough to get out before bringing kids into that…mess."

"Oh, I don't know if it's the same thing. I saw your parents together. If they were ever in love, it wasn't there by the time they started coming up here in the summers. You and Cole on the other hand…" Carol shrugged.

"Me and Cole what?"

"There's still feelings there. Whether you believe it or not." Carol put the potatoes in the oven beside a chicken roasting on the middle rack.

"That's just because he doesn't want to accept that it's over." Emily took the colander to the sink and ran cool water over the green beans.

"If you ask me, he's not the only one who still cares." Carol put her back to the counter and faced Emily. "I've seen the way you look at him."

Heat rushed to Emily's face. "That's just the hormones." Even as she said the words, though, she knew there was more involved than a rush of hormonal input. She'd kissed him back, with as much desire and depth as he had kissed her. The familiar rush of heat had risen in her, and still simmered in her gut, even now.

She still cared about him, and always would. Love…

She'd avoid that word and combining it with the name Cole. Smarter to do that than to get wrapped up in a fantasy, instead of reality.

Carol just *hmm*ed at that and started the dishes. Emily picked up a dish towel to help dry, but Carol shooed her away. "You're still a guest here, missy. So go do what guests do and relax."

Emily headed outside, forgetting until she heard the tapping of a hammer on nails that Cole was out here, working. Still. She started to turn around and head back into the inn when Cole called out to her.

"Hey, do you mind helping me for a second?" he said. "I could really use a second pair of hands."

He was holding a long board in one hand, a hammer in the other. With the tool belt slung across his hips and sawdust peppering his jeans and work boots, he looked relaxed. Sexy.

A few minutes of helping Cole would be

about being nice, not about getting close to him and admiring his body. Or the heat that still rushed through her veins whenever he was near.

"What do you need?" she asked.

"Just hold one end in place. I'm trying to get the rest of the siding repaired on this side of the building, but first I have to fit this fascia board in place."

She stared at him. They'd built the New York house from the ground up, and though Emily had been in charge of the decisions about faucets and paint colors, Cole had handled all the construction details, because he had spent so many years working on houses and knew the lingo. "Fascia board?"

"It goes up there." Cole pointed to the roofline ten feet above them.

She couldn't see any way that Cole could do this job alone, not without risking a broken neck. "Okay. Just don't ask me to hammer. You know how I am with tools."

"Oh, I remember, Emily." He winked at her. "My thumb remembers, too."

"Sorry." She grinned. "Again."

Cole got on one of the ladders and waited for Emily to get on the other one. They stepped up in tandem, until he had the board in place under the gutter and she had aligned her edge with the roofline.

"I'm just teasing you about my thumb," he said with a smile. "It wasn't so bad."

"That's not what you said that day. All we were doing was hanging some pictures, and you made it into a major project. Tape measure, level, laying out the frame placement with masking tape. Our house wasn't the Louvre, you know." She grinned.

"So I'm a little anal about those kinds of things."

"A little?" She arched a brow.

"Okay, a lot. I guess I deserved having you hit my thumb with the hammer."

"Well, as long as we're admitting weaknesses, I guess I was a little impatient. I just wanted the whole thing to be done." She shrugged. "I could have gone slower, and maybe not given you a hammer whack in the process."

"Even if I deserved it?"

She laughed. "Hey, you said it, not me."

He fiddled with the board, aligning it better, then grabbing a nail out of the tool belt and sinking the first one into the plywood. "You know, I think that was the last time we ever worked together on something."

"It was." Emily shifted her weight. A wave of light-headedness hit her, but she shrugged it off. "It's no wonder. That day didn't go very well." It had ended with a fight and Cole sleeping on the couch, too, but Emily didn't mention that. They had an easy détente between them now, and she wanted to preserve that peace a while longer.

"True," he said softly. "Let's hope this goes better."

"It should." She grinned. "We're on opposite ends of the board."

Cole laughed, then dug in his tool belt for a few more nails, hammering them in one at a time. "All appendages accounted for?" he asked her.

"Yup." The light-headedness hit her again, and she leaned into the ladder, shifting her grip on the board again. "You almost done?"

"A few more nails. Hold on a second. I have to move my ladder down toward you." He climbed down, shifted the ladder a few feet forward, then climbed back up and started hammering again.

A wave of nausea and dizziness slammed into Emily. She closed her eyes, but it didn't ease the feeling. Her face heated, she swayed again. All she wanted was to get off this ladder. Now.

"Cole, I...I need to get down." She let go of the board, gripped the ladder and climbed down to the ground. The light-headedness persisted so she sat on the edge of the porch, under the cool shadow of the overhang.

In an instant, Cole was there, the board forgotten, his voice filled with concern. "Hey, you okay?"

"Yeah, yeah. Just got a little dizzy being up so high."

"Then you sit. Or, if you want, go inside. I can handle this. The hard part is all done."

"I'm fine. Just give me a minute." She waved him off, part of her wanting him to hold her close and tell her it was all okay, the other part wishing he would go away and leave her be. Heck, wasn't that how she had felt for the past six months? Torn between wanting him close and wanting him gone.

It was as if she couldn't quite give up on the dream. Couldn't let go of the hope that this could all work out. Their marriage was like the Gingerbread Inn, Emily realized. In desperate need of major repairs and a lot of TLC.

The only difference? The inn wasn't past

the point of no return yet. Their marriage, on the other hand, was. If anything told her that, it was the conversation the other night about kids where Cole made it clear he wasn't on the same page as she was. Now she was having a baby her husband didn't want, and the sooner she accepted that, the better. Besides, any change in him this week was temporary. She knew that from experience. At the first sign of trouble at the company, Cole would be gone, for weeks on end, and she'd be on her own.

"Are you sure you're okay?" Cole asked. "You look a little pale."

"Yeah, yeah, I'm fine." *Just a little pregnant, is all.*

He looked like he wanted to probe deeper. Instead, Cole cleared his throat and shifted the hammer in his hand. He glanced up at the fascia board they'd installed, then back at Emily. "I, uh, better finish up."

She shifted to the side so he could climb up the ladder and finish hammering in the wood. By the time the last nail was in, Emily had gone inside. Because staying out there watching Cole fix the inn she loved only made her long for the impossible.

* * *

Cole's back ached, his shoulders burned and his legs hurt more than after his thrice-weekly run. His hands had calluses and nicks, and a fine shadow of stubble covered his jaw. When he looked in the mirror, he saw a man as far from a billionaire CEO as one could get.

It felt good. Damned good.

Still, he was smart enough to know he couldn't stay here forever. He had a business to get back to, a business that needed his attention. Every day he spent away from WTD was one that impacted the bottom line. People depended on him—*families* depended on him— to keep the profits coming so they could pay their mortgages and put food on their tables. Instead, he was here, working on the Gingerbread Inn, a place that meant something to Emily.

Because he'd thought they stood a chance. After that kiss, hope had filled him. Hope they could find their way back as a couple if they just spent more time together. But it seemed every time they got close, she put up this wall. Or she walked away, shutting the door as effectively with her distance as she had the day she'd asked him to move out of their house.

Did she have a point? Was it all about not

wanting to give up? Admit defeat? Was it about the battle, not about love?

His phone vibrated against his hip. Cole flipped it out, shifting from carpenter mode to businessman in an instant. He dropped onto the bottom step, and for the next half hour, worked out the details of a deal with a partner in China, made a decision about firing a lackluster employee and hammered out the contents of the quarterly investor report with Irene, his assistant.

"The place is going nuts without you," Irene said. "You'd think the sun had stopped shining or something."

Cole ran a hand through his hair. This was why he rarely took vacations and worked most weekends. "I'll come back in the morning."

"You will do no such thing." Irene's calm voice came across the line strong and sure. In her sixties, Irene had always been more than an assistant—she'd been a guiding force, a sort of mother not just to Cole but to everyone at WTD. She was plainspoken and filled with common sense, so when she talked, Cole knew he'd do well to listen.

"And why would I stay here when the company is in a panic?"

"Because it'll do all the lemmings around

here some good to take on a little leadership. And because it'll do you even more good to do something other than wither away under the fluorescent lighting."

He chuckled. "I am far from withered away, Irene."

"You go entire days without seeing the sunshine. You're here before me, stay long after those with common sense go home. You need to notice the world around you, not just the workload before you."

Wasn't that what Emily had said a hundred times over the years? She'd told him he worked too many hours, was home too few. He'd insisted the company needed him, but maybe it was something more, something deeper inside himself that kept him behind that desk day after day instead of with his wife, enjoying the life he had worked so hard to afford.

Irene had a point. If he took a few days off, then maybe the so-called lemmings he'd hired would step up to the plate and do what he'd hired them to do—lead in his stead. Rather than everyone looking to Cole because he was always there in the driver's seat.

"I'm doing that now."

"Are you? Because I'll bet dollars to doughnuts that you haven't heard those birds chirping in the background or the soft whistle of the breeze through the trees. How about the sun? Is it shining bright, or is it dimmed by cloud cover?"

Cole raised his gaze and squinted. "Bright." His gaze skimmed over the pale blue sky, then down the trees, almost bare now that November was edging toward December. Birds flitted from branch to branch, determined to stay as long as they could before caving to winter's cold. The breeze danced in the last few dangling leaves, waving them like flags. Through the trees, he could see the lake, glistening and inviting while squirrels dashed to and fro, making last-minute preparations for winter. He paused a long moment, letting the day wash over him and ease the tension in his shoulders. "You're right. I never noticed any of that."

"And you need to, Cole. Before it's too late."

"It might already be." He let out a long breath. Irene was the only one who knew about his marital problems. As his right-hand person at WTD, she had seen the end of his marriage coming long before he had. She'd noticed that there'd been fewer and fewer lunches with Emily, more long days when he didn't leave before dark and more weekends spent at the office instead of at home. He'd also given Irene a heads-up about the projects he was working on—both the one with the inn and the one with his marriage.

"Has she kicked you out of that inn yet?" Irene asked. "Told you to leave?"

"Not yet." Though, given her reaction to their kiss, Cole wasn't so sure Emily wanted him around anymore. She hadn't said that out loud yet, but he'd sensed a distance, a wall whenever he got too close. Like when she'd felt ill and he'd asked her if she was okay—Emily had suddenly gone cold and distant.

"If she hasn't kicked you out, then it's not too late. Now get your head out of the office and pay attention to what's around you," Irene said. "I'll handle things here. We'll all be fine."

He chuckled. "Is that an order?"

"You bet your sweet bippy it is. Now let me go so I can get some work done around here. Not all of us can sit around in the sun, listening to the birds chirp, you know." Her words lacked any bite and held only affection and worry.

"Thanks, Irene," Cole said, his voice quiet and warm.

"Anytime, Cole. Anytime." Then she was

gone. Cole tucked the phone back into his pocket.

He started to get to his feet, to get back to working on the fascia and soffits. He paused. Looked up at the sky, then sat back down, leaned against the porch post, closed his eyes and drew in the scents and sounds of the world he had missed for too many years.

CHAPTER SIX

EMILY STOOD ON the porch for a good minute, sure she was seeing things. Cole sat on the top step, his back against one of the thick posts, his face upturned to the sun. Asleep. Harper lay on the weathered boards beside Cole, eyes closed, tail tapping a slow, happy rhythm.

Emily smiled. Her workaholic husband, taking a break. Something she hadn't seen in so long, she'd been half-sure he was a robot, not a man. In sleep, he looked younger, boyish almost, with his face relaxed, his shoulders untensed.

Like the man she used to know. The man she had fallen in love with.

Her hand strayed to her abdomen, and for a second, she allowed herself to picture Cole's face when she told him about the baby. To imagine a future where he brought them home from the hospital, and they formed a little family of three.

Then Cole's phone started buzzing, the screen lighting with yet another call. A dose of reality inserting itself before she got wrapped up in a fantasy.

Carol came out on the porch. "He's asleep?" she whispered.

Emily nodded. "Doesn't happen very often."

Carol chuckled. "I've known men like that. Would rather work themselves half to death than admit they need a nap. Or a helping hand. I tell you, men are some of God's most stubborn creatures."

Emily laughed. "I agree with that."

The buzzing at his waist finally roused Cole. He jerked upright, disoriented for a second, reaching for the phone with an instinct well honed over the years. Just before he pressed the button to answer it, he noticed Emily and Carol, and set the phone back in the holster. "Sorry, I, uh, guess I fell asleep."

Cole ignoring a work call? And taking a nap in the middle of the day? That made for two miracles in the space of a few minutes—and two things Emily never thought she'd see.

"You're human...sleep happens." Carol smiled. "Either way, I'm glad you woke up. Dinner's in the kitchen and just waiting for some hungry people to come along."

Cole got to his feet and brushed the sawdust off his jeans. "A home-cooked meal? Can't remember the last time I had one of those."

"That's because you have to be home to have one." The words slipped from Emily's lips before she could stop them. Sometimes it seemed the years of resentment lay in wait behind paper walls, waiting for any small opening.

"You're right." Cole paused beside her on the porch. His blue eyes met hers. "But I also have to have a home to go to."

She shook her head and looked away before the familiar argument about their separation sprang up between them on this pretty fall day. She didn't want to fight anymore. Not one more disagreement. She'd had enough of those to last her a lifetime.

"Let's not do this," Cole said, as if he'd read her mind. "It's too nice of a day to argue about anything other than whether the sky is a cerulean-blue or cornflower-blue."

She smiled. "Cornflower. Definitely."

"I agree," Cole said.

Carol put a hand on each of their shoulders. "There's a home here, and a meal, and both of you are invited to the table if you promise to mind your manners."

Cole grinned. "Yes, ma'am."

Maybe it was the way he said *ma'am,* or maybe it was the way he smiled, but Emily found her anger melting in the light of both, and she paused in the doorway to shoot Cole a conspiratorial smile. "That means no food fights, you know."

"Too bad." He leaned in toward her, smelling of soap and sunshine. "Because sometimes cleaning up afterward can be a hell of a lot of fun."

"I remember." The words whispered into the small space between them, the memory charging the air. They'd come home from their quick three-day honeymoon to the tiny one-bedroom apartment that had been their first home. She'd worked half the day on a dinner for her new husband, poring over a cookbook she'd got out of the library, fixing chicken and peas and baked potatoes, then attempting a chocolate cream pie because he'd once said that was his favorite. "I really messed that meal up, didn't I?"

He chuckled as he followed her into the inn and down the long hall toward the dining room that flanked the western side of the house and looked out over the lake. "It wasn't *that* awful."

"Your memory is faulty. The chicken was burned, the peas shriveled and dried, and the potatoes undercooked." She shook her head. "But you ate every bite."

"Couldn't disappoint my new wife and tell her that she couldn't cook."

"I *still* can't cook." That had been the one benefit to Cole's sizable income—the convenience of ordering already-made meals. Emily vowed to learn to cook before the baby came. She imagined herself baking cookies and whipping up macaroni and cheese, with Sweet Pea helping measure and stir. Emily would never be Betty Crocker, but if she could at least master the basics, she could create the kind of warm, cozy home she'd always wanted.

"You might not be able to cook," Cole said. "But you can make a pie that sticks to my forehead."

She laughed. The laughter felt good, and she realized it had been far too long since she'd had a damned good laugh. "I didn't mean to throw it at you, but when you ate it like it was the most delicious pie you ever ate, I got so mad."

"It *was* the most delicious pie I ever ate, Emily."

They had stopped outside the dining room, lingering by the doorway while Carol put the finishing touches on the table. Harper sat in the corner, waiting and hoping for a scrap.

Emily stood within inches of Cole. Close enough to touch, to see the gold flecks in his eyes, to get wrapped up in the tempting scent of his cologne, the draw of his warm body. She moved away, headed for the table before she did any of those foolish things.

"How could you say that pie was good?" She reached for the pile of silverware on the corner and placed it beside the place settings. Avoiding the desire washing over her, the need to kiss him again, as strong as when they'd first dated. Damn. When would she stop wanting Cole? The separation and divorce would be much easier if her body got on board with her brain. "I forgot the sugar. That was the worst pie ever."

Cole slipped in beside her, tucking the folded napkins under the knives. "It was the most delicious pie ever, Emily," and he paused a beat until she looked up at him, "because you made it with love."

She held his gaze for a long moment, then shook her head and stepped away. Oh, how she wanted to believe in that look in his eyes, the words he spoke, but she was afraid, so afraid, that if she did, they'd end up traveling the same path as before. They'd done it countless times over the years. Now, with a baby caught in the mix, Emily couldn't afford to hold on to a fairy tale that she knew had an unhappy ending.

"Unfortunately, you need more ingredients than love to hold a recipe together and make it work," she said and turned away before he saw the tears brimming in her eyes.

Cole had to admire Carol, the inn's owner. She could have brokered a Middle East peace treaty with ease. She'd sensed the tension between Cole and Emily the instant she sat down at the table, and managed to shift the conversation to subjects that kept the room feeling light and lively. As they ate, they talked about the weather, the repairs to the inn, the Patriots' chances of making it to the Super Bowl. Fun, easy, small talk.

"Did Emily ever tell you the story about the lake's history?" Carol asked Cole as she laid warm plates of homemade apple pie before them. Melting scoops of vanilla ice cream puddled over the flaky crust. The impressive dessert could have starred on a magazine cover.

Emily let out a little laugh. "Oh, not this one. It's not even true."

"It is, too," Carol said, then grinned. "Or at least partly true."

"Let me guess," Cole said. Even though he was stuffed from the amazing roast chicken, potatoes and green beans, he dived into the pie with gusto. "Barrow's Lake has its own resident Loch Ness monster?"

"No, no, though that might draw in more visitors, and that'd be good for business." Carol put a finger on her lips. "Hmm…if only I could buy a Loch Ness monster in the pet store."

"Two words," Cole said. "Inflatable toy."

"I'll keep that in mind for the summer tourists." Carol laughed. "Well, our lake story is a little more innocuous. Way back, years ago, before the invention of the car—"

"When dinosaurs roamed the earth," Emily added.

"Well, maybe not that far back in time. But close." Carol leaned forward, her eyes bright with excitement as she told the story. "There used to be two families, one on either side of the lake, one with a daughter, one with a son, about the same age. They didn't know each other, and in these years when this area was just beginning to get settled by people in wagons and log homes, there was no Facebook or Skype or high school to bring them together. Then John Barrow, one of the original Barrows to settle here, opened a little store smack-dab in the center of the road between the two families. You can still see the remains of its foundation, past that big pine tree." She pointed out the window. "The shop wasn't much, just a general sundries kind of place. The teenagers ran into each other there one summer day, and fell in love. They'd meet at the store every afternoon after they finished their chores and spend time together. But the families were at war over something no one can remember now, and the teens were forbidden from seeing each other."

"Nevertheless, they sneaked away every afternoon," Emily put in, "because they were deeply in love and couldn't bear to be apart."

"That's right. Sometimes true love is stronger than parental rule." Carol grinned. "And that was how it was for these two. But oh, the ruckus it raised in their families. So one stormy fall night, they made plans to run away and get married. Before they could leave, their parents found out and rushed down to the store to interrupt the rendezvous. The kids panicked, took a boat and rowed out to the middle of the lake, thinking they could make it across and leave from the other side. The storm that night was strong, and the water rough, and the boat capsized. Sadly, both kids drowned."

"That's terrible," Cole said. Even though the event had happened decades ago, he could imagine the heartbreak and loss, particularly on such a small community. "How devastating for those families."

"It was an awful tragedy, and one that haunted this area for years." Carol gestured toward the moon-kissed lake outside the windows. "There are people who say you can still see the ghosts of the doomed lovers in the fog that rises over the lake at night."

"And according to Carol, if you're out in that fog, you're destined to fall in love." Emily grinned. "When us girls were teenagers, we'd run outside if we saw the fog, but none of us fell in love with the boys here for the summer."

"That's because none of them were right for you," Carol said. "You have to be with the right one for the fog to work."

Emily laughed and got to her feet, grabbing the empty plates as she did. "And all the stars and moon have to be aligned just right, too. It's a legend, Carol, and not one I believe in."

Carol wagged a finger at her. "You'll see. Some foggy night, true love will come your way."

Emily didn't answer that. Instead, she brushed open the swinging door with her hip and set the plates in the sink, then filled it with soapy water. By the time she returned, Cole and Carol were talking about the repairs on the Inn, instead of silly age-old legends.

Just as well. The last thing she needed Cole to do was drag her down to the lake in the middle of the night because he believed some legend about dead teenagers would fix their marriage. No kiss on a foggy night was going to repair the damage the years of distance had created.

Maybe if they had gone to counseling when the problems first started, it would have righted the ship's course. She'd asked Cole to go, but time and time again, Cole had put off the appointment. She'd given up after a while and stopped asking him. If their marriage was important to him, she'd reasoned, he would have made the time to save it.

Then again, she hadn't gone on her own, either, or fought very hard to get Cole to the appointments. She'd been just as guilty about finding other things to fill her time. Maybe because deep down she was afraid to confront the issues between them—and find out they were beyond fixing.

"You know, Cole, it doesn't make much sense for you to drive all the way into the city tonight," Carol was saying as Emily picked up the platter of chicken, "when I have rooms right upstairs. Why don't you stay here? It's the least I can do to thank you."

Cole stay here? Emily prayed he'd say no, that he would do what he always did, say he needed to leave in the morning to get back to the office. But no, he grinned and nodded instead. Damn. Having him stay here was a definite complication, especially to her hormones and her heart. She needed to stay firm in her resolve and not be swayed by a smile.

"That'd be great, Carol. I'll have my luggage sent over in the morning." Cole rose, stretched his back and let out a yawn. "Just the thought of driving back to the hotel makes me exhausted."

"Well, I'm exhausted just hearing you talk about it." Carol gave the two of them a smile. "I hate to ask this, but I'm really tired. Lots of early mornings and a little stress over this renovation/sale thing. Would you two mind clearing up the rest of the dishes? I'd like to get to bed early."

Emily shot Carol a curious look, but the innkeeper just muffled a yawn and kept her gaze averted. Emily suspected Carol of a little matchmaking, what with telling the story of the two doomed lovers and asking Cole to stay at the inn. Maybe with Carol out of the room, Emily could make Cole see that his being here wasn't a good idea. "No problem. See you in the morning, Carol."

Carol thanked them, then hurried out of the room. Harper stayed behind, ever hopeful for scraps. Cole and Emily gathered the rest of the dishes and brought them into the kitchen. "You don't have to help," Emily said to Cole as she slipped on an apron and tied it behind her back. "I know how you hate doing dishes."

He shrugged. "I used to hate it. Now I've kind of gotten used to it."

"You're doing your own dishes?" She shot him a glance. In his jeans and T-shirt, he looked like a guy who did his own dishes, a million miles away from the wealthy, driven CEO. "You're not having a maid do them?"

"It's not like I cook a gourmet meal every night," Cole said. "I usually have one plate, one cup and a fork to wash. No need to pay the maid to do that."

"Yeah, me, too." She'd let the household

help go, too, after their separation. She'd seen no sense in paying people to clean up after one person. Plus doing her own housework kept her busy instead of focusing on how Cole's absence made the house echo in ways it never had before.

"Nothing drives home the fact that you're alone like washing your dishes." Cole took the clean dishes from the strainer, swiped them dry with a towel and put them in the cabinets. "I guess that's when it finally hit me."

"What did?" Emily stowed the leftovers in the fridge.

Cole put his back to the sink and crossed his arms over his chest, the pink-and-white-striped towel a strange juxtaposition in his muscular hands. "That this wasn't a fight we'd get over in a couple days. That this separation could be permanent. I'd come home from work and look at that plate and cup and fork in the sink and think…" He let out a gust and shook his head. "I'd think how sad they looked."

"Really?" Over the years, Cole had rarely opened up about his feelings. She'd asked him what he was thinking, but most of the time, he'd withdrawn and in the end, she'd be left feeling cold, alone. This was the most he'd shared in a long, long time.

"All those years we lived together, I don't think I ever noticed if we had five plates or fifty," he went on. "I couldn't tell you what the pattern was on our silverware if you paid me. But I notice the plates now. I notice when there's one." He nodded toward the sink. "Or more than one."

Her heart softened. She put the empty serving dishes in the soapy water, then picked up one of the plates and started washing it, instead of falling into that vulnerable look on Cole's face and in his voice. "I notice now, too," she said quietly. "It's like the plate and cup are lonely."

"Maybe I should buy a whole set." Cole grinned. "Or just bring mine back home so they'd be together again. Happy. Complete."

The thought of him returning, of the two of them being happy and complete, together again, caused her heart to race and her throat to close. Hope warred with caution. She concentrated on getting the plate clean, watching the bubbles circle and circle the rim. "We've tried that before, Cole. It didn't work."

"What's that saying about success? That it's about not giving up?"

She could see the saying now, one of those kitschy posters that she had hung in her college dorm, then again in their run-down first apartment because it was the only wall decor they could afford. By the time they moved to the big house, the poster had been relegated to a landfill. But the saying and the image of a determined competitor in a tough tug-of-war had stuck with Emily. "'Success seems to be largely a matter of hanging on after others have let go.' William Feather said it," she said.

"I'm hanging on, Emily," Cole said softly. "I really am."

She placed the clean plate in the strainer, then picked up the next one. "Why?"

"Because we had something once. And I think we can have it again. And because I'm ready for change."

How she wanted to believe him. Her brain reminded her heart that he had said all this before, and gone back to his workaholic ways as soon as the crisis passed. How could she know this time would be any different?

Another clean plate in the strainer. She tackled the third one. The only sound in the room was the running water and the soft clanging of dishes. "Change how?"

"Working less. More vacations. More time for you and me to get back to where we were."

She'd heard all these words before. Dozens

of times over the years, and every time, she had believed them, only to be hurt in the end. Granted, the time he had spent working on the repairs to the inn was the most time he'd ever taken off work before, and maybe that meant something. Maybe it meant he had changed. Hope kept a stubborn hold on her heart, but she refused to give it space and room.

Not until she'd asked the most important question.

She rinsed the last plate, put it in the strainer, then tackled a pan, keeping her gaze away from Cole's. "And what about a family?"

He let out a nervous laugh. "Family? Emily, we're *far* from ready for kids."

It's what he'd said a thousand times over the years. Every time she'd brought up kids, he'd said it wasn't the right time, or that they'd talk about it later. She pulled the plug, let the soapy water drain, and placed her hands on the rim of the sink. All that silly, foolish hope in her chest drained away, too.

"When *do* you think we'll be ready? When we get a bigger house or the company reaches another sales goal or we have another million saved in retirement?" She snorted and turned away from him. "It's never the right time, Cole."

"We're a few pieces of paper away from being divorced, Emily. I'd say that's the worst possible time to have a child."

Emily sighed. "Yeah, Cole, it is." Then she left the kitchen and headed up to her room, where the pillow would muffle her hurt.

CHAPTER SEVEN

COLE SLEPT THROUGH his alarm. Slept through the buzzing of his phone. Slept through the sunrise. He'd slept in the best hotel rooms in the world, owned a mattress that cost more than a small car, and yet he had never slept as soundly or as well as he had in the double bed in the pale blue room on the second floor of the Gingerbread Inn.

He rolled over, blinked a bleary eye at his phone and decided whoever was calling him could wait a little longer. This...decadence filled him with a peace he had never felt before. Whatever was happening at work would be there later, while Cole just...was. Right here, right now, in a cozy bedroom across the hall from Emily, in a quaint inn in Massachusetts. He lay in the bed, watching the sun dance on the floor, while birds chirped a song above the faint sounds of a distant lawn mower.

Then he heard the soft melody of a woman's

voice, singing along with the radio. It took him a moment to realize it was Emily's voice. He hadn't heard her singing in...

Hell, ten years. At least.

He pulled on his jeans and padded barefoot out of his room and across the hall. Her door stood ajar, the bed made, the room neat and clean. When had Emily become a neatnik? She'd always been the messier one in their relationship, something that had driven him crazy when they were together. Then, when he was on his own, he'd missed seeing her makeup on the bathroom counter, her coat tossed over the dining room chair, her shoes kicked off on the bedroom carpet. He'd tried leaving his own things out but it wasn't the same. He hesitated only a moment, then took a single step inside the room. "Em?"

The bedroom was empty. Light and steam spilled out of the attached bathroom. The shower was running, and Cole could see the familiar outline of his wife's curves behind the translucent white curtain. Desire rushed through him, hardened against his jeans. How long had it been since he'd been with Emily?

Months. Three, to be exact. A long damned time.

He hesitated. He knew he should leave but

couldn't tear his gaze away from her shapely outline, the curve of her breasts, her hips. She was hidden by the curtain, yet he knew every dimple, every valley, every scar. He knew how to make her moan, how to make her smile, how to make her...

His.

Except she wasn't his anymore, and he needed to face that. Accept it. Move on.

Since the separation, he'd told himself he should take off his ring. Date again. But he hadn't. No woman had interested him the way his wife did. And maybe never would. He missed her, damn it, for more than just the warmth of her body against his.

The water stopped with a screech and a shudder of old pipes. Cole told himself to move. Leave. He didn't do either.

The song ended and a commercial came on the radio. Emily's voice trailed off as she reached up and tugged down the towel draped over the shower curtain. She jerked back the curtain and let out a shriek. "Cole! You scared me. What are you doing in here?"

Shit. He should have left. Now he looked like some overeager hormonal teenager, which was how he felt whenever he was around Emily. Even now, even after everything.

"Your, uh, door was open. And I heard you singing and…" He forced his gaze up from the hourglass shape outlined by the fluffy white towel. "I can't remember the last time I heard you singing."

A flush filled her cheeks and her gaze shifted to the floor. "I'm a terrible singer."

"Didn't sound that way to me. It was nice." He swallowed hard. "I've missed your singing. You used to sing all the time when we were first married."

She laughed. "That's because we couldn't even afford a TV. My singing was our only entertainment."

"I wouldn't say it was our *only* entertainment." His gaze met hers. Heat filled the space between them. Cole had never been so acutely aware of his wife's naked body, and the thin scrap of cotton separating them. She'd put on a few pounds in the past couple months, but they only added to her curves and made her more desirable. He ached to take her in his arms, to let the towel fall to the floor and to taste that sweet, warm, peach skin.

"Those were different days then," she said, her voice low and soft. She fiddled with the edge of the towel. "Better days."

Had she stopped singing because she'd

stopped being happy? Started again today because she was happier without him? Or had he stopped paying attention to Emily so long ago that he didn't notice her singing? Her happiness?

"You liked it better when we were poor?" he asked. "Living in that tiny fifth-floor walkup, freezing in the winter and roasting in the summer?"

"Yeah, I did."

He'd hated those days. Always struggling, feeling like he'd failed, the constant battle to get his business off the ground at night while he sweated on a construction site during the day. Working, working, working, and getting frustrated at how long it took to get from nowhere to somewhere. "Why? We had nothing, Emily."

"Nothing except each other," she said. She raised her gaze to his. Tears shimmered in her green eyes. "That was always enough for me, Cole. But it was never enough for you."

He let out a gust. Why did it always come down to this? Didn't she understand, he'd done all of this for her? For them? For their future together? The hours he'd worked, the effort he'd put in to take the business from their apartment kitchen table to a global power had been a constant source of friction between them. In the early days, Emily had supported him, but as the years wore on, that support had eroded into frustration and a cold, silent war.

"You can't blame me for wanting more, Emily. For wanting success. Look at us now. We have everything we always wanted."

A bittersweet smile crossed her face. "No. You have everything *you* ever wanted." The smile shifted, became something he couldn't read, as if Emily had a secret that only she knew. She nodded toward the door. "I'd appreciate it if you left now."

He did as she asked and left the room, shutting the door behind him, and feeling more lost than he had ever felt before. Cole was a smart man who had built his company from nothing into a global player. Who had taken them from a run-down apartment to a mansion in a tony suburb outside New York City. All along, he'd thought he was on the same path that Emily wanted.

Now it turned out he'd been wrong. For a long, long time.

Sleep eluded Emily. She tossed and turned, then got up, tried to write and couldn't get any further in the book. The whole day had been like that, her creativity stalled. Her mind was still stuck on the moment Cole had walked into the bathroom and looked at her with that hungry, admiring gaze she knew so well. One step forward, and she would have had him in her arms, in her bed, in her.

She craved that, deep down inside, in places that only Cole knew. But she'd held her ground, and after he left the room, she'd told herself she'd done the right thing. Even if it didn't feel that way.

Her stomach rumbled. She pulled on a robe and headed downstairs to the kitchen. The inn was silent, and only a small light burned on the kitchen table. Moonlight streamed in through the windows, providing enough light for her to make her way through the rooms.

Emily pulled open the fridge, and mulled over the choices. She settled on the leftover apple pie. A second later, she was dishing a hearty slice onto a small dessert plate. After all, she was eating for two now. She could afford an extra serving of dessert once in a while. She heard a sound and looked up to find Cole standing in the kitchen.

He wore only a pair of old gray sweatpants that she knew well. He'd had them for as long as she could remember, the fleece worn and soft as butter. His chest was bare, and the desire that had been burning inside her all day roared to life again. Her hand flexed at her side, itching to touch the hard muscular planes, to draw his warmth to her.

"Great minds think alike," Cole said, taking a step closer and gesturing toward the pie.

"Do you want a piece?" Then she looked down and realized she'd taken the last of the pie. "Sorry. Um, would you like to share?"

"If you don't mind."

"Not at all." She pulled open the drawer and handed a second fork to Cole. He leaned over one side of the kitchen island, she leaned over the other side and they each took a bite of the pie. Their heads were so close, they nearly touched. It was so much like the early days, when they'd been inseparable and in love, that Emily could almost believe she'd gone back in time. She ached to run her fingers through Cole's dark hair, to kiss the crumbs off his lips, to giggle when his shadowy stubble tickled her chin.

"Carol's pies are legendary," she said instead.

"I can see why."

Emily forked up another bite. "The other Gingerbread Girls and I would sneak down here in the middle of the night all the time and eat the leftovers. She'd yell at us in the morning, but half the time she was laughing at the same time. And sometimes she'd bake an extra pie, just so we'd have one to scavenge."

"Those must have been some amazing summers," Cole said.

"They were. Some of my best memories are wrapped up in this place." She sighed. "I'm going to hate to see it sold off and turned into condos or something awful like that."

He scooped up some ice cream. "Why don't I buy it? Let Carol run it…keep things as they are."

Emily let out a gust. She put her fork down and leaned away from the counter. "Not everything can be fixed with money, Cole."

"I'm just trying to help."

She read honesty in his face, and relaxed. He had helped over the past few days, more than he knew. She couldn't fault him for wanting to do more. After all, finding solutions to impossible situations was Cole's specialty. He'd built a business on designing creative answers to customer problems.

For years, he'd been the one she relied on to solve everything from a checking account error to a strange noise coming from her engine. For the past six months, she'd relied only on herself. As scary as it had been, the independence had given her a newfound confidence. It was a feeling she wanted to keep, which meant no more running to Cole to fix the things that went awry. "Listen, I appreciate all the help you're giving Carol with the repairs, I really do."

"But...?"

She forked up some pie, but didn't eat it. Instead, she turned to the fridge. "Do you want some milk?"

"Yes," he said, coming around the counter to face her, "but I also want you to tell me what you aren't saying."

She grabbed the gallon jug, then two glasses, and poured them each an icy glass of milk. She slipped onto one of the bar stools and wrapped her hands around the glass. She debated whether to tell him what she was thinking, then decided she'd done enough of ignoring the issues, and maybe it was time to speak up instead of letting those thoughts simmer. "You have a tendency to throw money at a problem and then leave," she said. "At least when it comes to us."

He dropped into the opposite bar stool. "I don't do that."

"When something needed fixing at the house, you called someone to do it. When I needed to buy a new car, you called a friend at a dealership and had him show me the newest models. When I wanted to go on a vacation, you called a travel agent and told her to send me anywhere I wanted to go."

"What's wrong with that? It's problem solving."

Emily bit her lip, then raised her gaze to his. "The problem wasn't the leaky faucet or the old car or the need for some time in the sun. It was that I wanted to do those things with you, Cole. I wanted *you and me* to install that faucet, even if it was messy and frustrating and time-consuming to do it. I wanted *you* to go with me to pick out a car, and go along on the test drive, and give me your opinion, then laugh when I bought what was prettiest. I wanted *you* to go on vacation with me and—" she exhaled "—just be. You and me for a few days."

He reached up and brushed a tendril of hair off her head. "I never knew, Emily. Why didn't you say anything?"

She slipped off the stool and away from his touch before she found herself in his arms again. In the darkened, silent room it was so tempting just to curve against Cole's bare chest and to forget the separation, the problems between them, the difficult road yet to come. Instead she crossed to the window and looked out over the darkened lake beyond the trees. "I could say that I never said anything because you were never home to talk to, but really, that's just an excuse. I never said anything because—" and now her throat swelled and tears rushed to her eyes "—I didn't want to hear you say no."

He was behind her in a second, wrapping her in his arms, and despite her resolve a second ago, she allowed herself to lean back into him, just this once, just for this minute. "I wouldn't have said no, Emily."

"Ah, but you did, Cole. A hundred times." She stepped out of his embrace, and turned to face him. "Every time we went our separate ways, you to work, me to my charity work and golf dates and all those meaningless things that filled the hours between breakfast and bed, it added a little distance to the gulf between us. Eventually, that gulf got too wide, Cole, and crossing it was a Herculean task." She shook her head. "I couldn't do it anymore."

He took in her words, then nodded. "And to be honest, I don't think I even realized that gulf existed until you asked for a separation. I had on these blinders that told me everything was just fine. When it was far from that."

"That was my fault, too. I didn't speak up." Emily flicked a crumb off the counter and watched it skitter into the sink. "When I was growing up, my parents fought all the time. If they were getting along, it made me nervous. It was like being around a purring tiger. You never knew when it would lash out again. That made me afraid to rock the boat, so I'd let things go that I should have done something about."

"I wish you had said something. I couldn't read your mind, Em. Though Lord knows I tried."

"Would you have listened?" She shifted closer to him. "You've been so dedicated to the company for so long that I don't think you would have heard me if I'd said the house was on fire."

"Well, I think I would have heard that." He chuckled, then sobered. "You're right. But you don't understand, Em. A company is like a puppy. It needs constant attention or it will wither and die."

"That's why you hire good people. To give you a break once in a while."

He shook his head. "You sound like Irene."

Emily raised a shoulder, dropped it again. "If everyone is saying the same thing, maybe they have a point."

"Or maybe none of them understand the demands on me as the owner. Being at the top is far more difficult than anyone understands." He let out a long sigh, then ran a hand through his hair. "Just when I think everything is under control and I can step back, something goes wrong. Hell, you wouldn't believe the number of calls and emails I've got just in the couple of days I've been here."

Tension had knotted his shoulders, furrowed his brow. The part of Emily that still cared about Cole filled with concern. She knew that look. Knew it well. She'd seen it hundreds of times. Before he had a team of employees under him, Cole would come home to their cramped apartment, a smokestack ready to blow, and she would be his sounding board. When had Cole stopped coming to her? When had she stopped asking him to share his day? "Do you want to talk about it?" she asked.

"You've got enough on your plate."

She could see him distancing himself, doing what he always did and taking all the problems on his shoulders. Putting another brick in the wall between them. Her first instinct was to throw up her hands and walk away, but really, had doing that made anything better?

Emily reached out and put a hand on his arm, a touch of comfort, but one that sent a zing through her. "Remember when we first got married and you were working around the clock, trying to pay the bills and launch the business?"

He nodded. "We'd stay up half the night, eating junk food and talking."

She laughed. "Kind of like we're doing tonight."

His gaze softened, and she let her touch drop away. "Yeah, kind of like tonight."

"Then why don't we sit down and talk it out? I may not know anything about technology, but I can be a good listener." *I'm still here, Cole,* she wanted to say. *I've always been here. Even if you stopped reaching out to me.* "I know you, Cole. If you're up in the middle of the night, it's because something is troubling you."

His features softened. "You still know me better than I know myself."

She didn't reply because a part of her felt like she didn't know him at all. Maybe they'd kept too much of themselves back for too long to ever find that connection again.

"Before I came down here, I was pacing my room, jotting down ideas, trying to figure out a solution to a problem at work." Then he waved it off. "But I don't want to keep you up, too. Go to bed, Em. I'll figure it out."

Maybe he'd stopped coming to her because she'd stopped asking. Stopped being there. Could he be caught in the same feeling of disconnect as she was?

Either way, she hated seeing this stress and tension on his face. She reached out and gave his hand a light touch. "Let's finish that pie and save the world. Or at least the world of Watson Technology Development."

"You sure you want me to bore you with the details?"

"I don't mind. If you want my opinion, that is."

"Of course I do, Em. You've always had great ideas when it came to the business. Maybe I should have hired you to work for me as a consultant."

She laughed. "That would have been a disaster."

"Maybe yes, maybe no." A tease lit his eyes. "Will you work on commission?"

She feigned deep thought. "Depends. Is there pie involved?"

"Always." He grinned. They crossed to the bar and took their seats again. The small kitchen light washed the room in a pale gold glow, while the moonlight added touches of silver. Outside, an owl hooted, but the world was quiet and still, except for this small corner of the Gingerbread Inn.

Cole steepled his fingers, a move Emily knew signaled he was getting serious. "I've got a huge order for the next generation of cell phones from one of my biggest customers. The launch is in place, the customer is ready for the rollout, but the product is delayed. We've had them under development for over a year, and things were on track, but then the plant that is making the screens was damaged in a storm. We found a backup supplier for the screens, but their quality hasn't been the best. So now we're stuck without a screen supplier, and the first order is due to drop in a week."

"All you have left to do is add the screens?"

He nodded. "If we had some to add, yes."

"Then do what you do best, Cole. Build it yourself." She tapped the counter before him. "Remember when you first started out, you had those prototype screens you made? You never used them because you found a supplier who could make them cheaper."

"That's right. They're still in the warehouse somewhere." He sat back, and Emily could see the wheels turning in Cole's head. "We could substitute those, at least for the first drop order, and that'll give the Japanese supplier time to get back online and ship the order to us." He gave his forehead a smack. "I can't believe I didn't think of it myself."

She shrugged. "Sometimes it's just a matter of hearing another opinion."

"A smart and wise opinion at that." He leaned back on the bar stool, his gaze skimming over her features. "I've missed hearing your opinion, Em. I guess I stopped asking. Or I stopped getting up in the middle of the night for pie."

If he had, would things be different? If he'd included her in the day-to-day of his company? Or asked her to do more than just attend another banquet or golf tournament? "It's been a long time since you asked what I think," she said.

"I'm sorry."

"Yeah, me, too."

The moment extended between them, full of regrets and missed opportunities. Cole was the first to look away, shifting his gaze to the plate before them. "Last bite. It's all yours. Payment for services rendered, as agreed."

"Oh, you can have it, Cole. I don't—"

He speared the last bit of pie, then held it before her lips. "I know you, Emily. And I know you want this."

His voice was low and dark, and sent a wave of temptation through her. Not for the pie— he was right, she always wanted pie—but for him. Damn. She'd always wanted him, too. No matter what.

She opened her lips and took the bite from him, slow, easy, their gazes locked, and the piece of pie became about much more than just some slices of cinnamon-glazed apples and flaky crust. Heat unfurled in her gut, and for a second she wished Cole would just lean her back against that counter and take her right here, right now. That it could be like it used to be, without the muddle of the past ten years.

"Delicious," he said. "Isn't it?"

"Very." She licked her lips and watched Cole watching her tongue. "Too bad it's all gone."

"Definitely too bad." Was she talking about the pie? Or the fact that she had enjoyed Cole feeding her? Enjoyed that one-on-one attention, like a laser?

The clock on the wall ticked by the wee hours. Somewhere outside, an owl hooted. Cole's eyes met Emily's. "Oh, Em, what are we doing here?"

"Having pie."

"And now that the pie is gone?"

He was talking about more than whether they were going to put the dish in the sink or grab another snack. Cole was asking her the one question she couldn't answer. What was going to happen next? With them?

As much as she wanted to believe they could take this moment and use it to rebuild their marriage, she was acutely aware that a new life was growing inside her. A child Cole didn't want.

She'd become a package deal, her and Sweet Pea. The problem was, Cole only wanted half the package.

She drew back. "I don't know, Cole. I really don't."

"Then let's leave it here, on this sweet, pie-flavored note." He quirked a grin in her direction. "Always leave them wanting more, isn't that the old saying?"

"And do you? Want more?" Damn it all, she still wanted him, still couldn't back away.

He cupped her jaw, his thumb tracing over her lips, following the path her tongue had taken. "God, yes," he said. "That's one thing that's never changed, Emily. I always want you. Always have. Always will."

That sent a little thrill through her, but she tamped it down. Desire was never their problem. She'd wanted him from the moment she'd met him, and still did. She drew in a breath, held it, then exhaled again, with a dose of clarity. "A marriage requires more than just sexual attraction."

He sat back on the stool. A whisper of cold air filled the space between them. "Then let's work on the other things a good marriage requires." She started to protest, but he held up a finger, stopping her. "We're here together for a few days at least, right? And yes, I know we're separated and a step away from divorced, but at the very least, let's try to learn how to connect with each other so that going forward, everything is amicable."

It made sense, though she doubted his motives were that simple. Cole had made it abundantly clear that he wanted to get back together and didn't want a divorce. At the same time, he'd made it clear he didn't want children.

Still, the part of her that had got up in the middle of the night, worried, scared and lonely, craved the connection they'd had in their early days. Would it be so bad to rely on him, just for a few days, especially as she got used to the idea of the changes that lay ahead for her? What could it hurt?

Or was she just looking for a reason to be close to the man who was no longer her perfect fit?

"Tell me," he said, draping an elbow over the bar, "what has you up in the middle of the night besides pie?"

"There are other reasons to get up besides sneaking the last piece of pie?" She grinned.

"I don't know. Pie's a pretty compelling reason." He leaned in closer to her, and for a second, she thought—no, hoped—he was going to kiss her. "So what's on your mind? I know you, Emily, and I know that look on your face. The way your brow furrows right there—" he laid a gentle finger on her temple "—tells me you're worried about something."

In that moment she wanted to tell Cole about the baby. Tell him how worried she was that she wouldn't be a good mother or that she would let the baby down somehow. A long time ago, Cole had been her best friend, the one she told everything to. But as they'd drifted apart, their friendship had eroded, and that, Emily knew, was what she mourned most about the end of her marriage.

Besides, if she told him about the baby, she knew how he'd react. He'd be angry that she had deviated from the careful plan they'd had. He didn't want kids now—and maybe not even later. He'd made that clear several times over the years and had reiterated the point the other day.

"I'm, uh, writing a book," she said. "I got a little writer's block and I was up, trying to figure out the next step in the plot."

He arched a brow in surprise. "You're writing a book?"

"I used to do that back in college, you know. I just put it aside for a while."

"I remember. Why?"

"What do you mean, why?"

"Why did you ever stop writing? You used to love doing it."

"Well, when we first got married, we were both working a crazy amount of hours while you got the business off the ground. Then once you were successful, my days got sucked up with things to support that." She fiddled with the fork, tapping it against the empty plate. "That's an excuse, really. I had the time, if I'd really wanted to find it. I just didn't."

"Why not?"

She raised a shoulder, dropped it. "I guess I was afraid. Once I finish a book, I have to send it out, and that..."

"Means you could get rejected."

She exhaled. "Yeah."

"But you've started now." Cole's hand covered hers. "That's all that matters. And if no publisher wants your book, I'll buy a printing press and—"

Emily jerked to her feet. Damn it. Why did he always return to the same answer? "Cole, I don't want you to solve my problems with money. I wasn't even asking you to solve it. I just wanted to talk, like you did with me, and have you listen, and most of all, let me find my own solution. If I get rejected, I get rejected. Maybe I'm not meant to be a writer. But you have to let me find that out instead of trying to fix everything with money."

"I don't do that."

"Yes, you do. When I was upset because my mother was moving to Florida, you bought her a house near ours. When I struggled to learn golf, you hired the best PGA coach in the business and flew him out to show me how to improve my swing. When I was sick with the flu, you had a doctor move into the guest room to be sure I was taken care of."

"That's what money buys, Emily. There's nothing wrong with that."

"Yeah, there is," she said. She put the dishes in the sink and propped her hands on either side. "It's the whole reason we're not together anymore, Cole. You talk about wanting to fix our relationship, about being a better husband, about being there for me. That was all I ever wanted, Cole, you. And what did I get instead?" She turned away from the sink. "Your checkbook."

"I was just trying to make things easier."

"Because it's easier to throw money at a problem than to actually get your hands—and your heart—into it." She shook her head, and wondered why she kept letting hope rise in her when they always circled back to the same disappointing end. Even if they stayed together and had the baby, she didn't need a crystal ball to predict the future. Cole would buy toys and trips to Disney World, but never be there for the first steps and soccer games. She let out a long, sad breath. "All I ever wanted was you."

Then she left the room, before the tears in her eyes spilled down her cheeks and told Cole the truth. That all she wanted now, *and always,* was him.

CHAPTER EIGHT

"A MAN COULD hurt himself doing that."

Cole turned at the familiar voice. Joe Bishop stood in the driveway of the Gingerbread Inn, grinning like a fool. Damn, it was good to see him. Cole notched the ax into the turned-over log beside him, then headed down the hill and over to his friend, one of the few people Cole had known since childhood. The two men exchanged a hearty hug while Harper barked and leaped around them, excited to see another newcomer. "I'm glad you're here, Joe. And not to help chop wood, though if you want to grab an ax, I won't stop you."

Joe laughed. "Count on you to show an old buddy a good time."

"Come on, let's get something to drink." Cole gestured to Joe to follow him. They circled around to the back door of the inn and went into the kitchen, where Cole pulled two icy beers out of the fridge and handed one to Joe. "We had some good times back in the day, more than one, if I remember right."

"If you're talking about your bachelor party," Joe said, "my memory of that night is a little fuzzy. In a good way."

Cole chuckled. "That was one wild night."

"Indeed. So was your wedding." Joe grinned. "That was, what, ten years ago? Every once in a while, I still think about that night. And the cute bartender I met." He winked. "Remember how she did that little shake when she mixed martinis? I think I ordered five of them just to see her shimmy."

Joe, still a ladies' man, the one in their group least likely to settle down. He'd started a landscaping business out of high school, and though he'd been successful enough to be able to expand and conquer the greater Boston area, Joe liked to keep his business small and manageable, so he could take off at a moment's notice for a weekend with a pretty woman.

"To unforgettable women," Cole said, tipping his bottle to connect with Joe's.

Joe took a long gulp. "Speaking of unforgettable women…how's Emily?"

The beer lost its appeal for Cole. He set his bottle on the steps, then sat down. How was

Emily? That was the million-dollar question. Last night, he'd thought they were making progress, getting close again. For a second, it had been like the old days when they were united by their struggles to get from nowhere to somewhere. Then somehow, the closeness derailed again.

He was missing something, some detail, but what it was, he couldn't say. Was it just about the money?

He used to think they both wanted success, but Emily seemed to resent the very thing he'd worked so hard to achieve. Admittedly, she had a point about him hiring people instead of doing the work himself. But a man could only spread himself so thin. Didn't she understand he'd done it to ease their lives rather than complicate them?

Cole shrugged. He had no answers last night, and he had fewer now. "She's here. I'm here. But it's like we're on different planets."

Joe sat on the step beside Cole. "Things have gotten that bad between you two?"

"There are times when I think we have a chance, then other times..." He shrugged. "Not so much. Maybe she's right."

"Right about what?"

"That I can't let go because I can't admit

I lost. That this is more about winning than about love."

Joe snorted. "That I can see. I have played racquetball with you, remember. I also recall one particularly crazy basketball game in your driveway. You are definitely a win-at-all-costs guy, Cole."

Cole cupped the beer between his palms and watched leaves flutter to the ground. In a couple of weeks, all would be bare here, covered with white, winter making its mark on the land around him. Even the trees caved to Mother Nature's power, giving up their leaves, their greenery, all their finery, to an enforced slumber that would last for the next three months.

"I think this time, that attitude is costing me my marriage. The problem? I honestly don't know if I can change. That's the very thing that's made me successful and what drives me every day. But it could also be the thing driving my wife away." He took a drink. "Maybe I should give her what she wants and leave."

"What does Emily say is the problem?"

"She says I try to solve everything with money rather than with just being there."

"And do you?"

"Well, yeah. But it's easier that way and leaves me time to—" Cole cut off the words and let out a curse. How could he have missed the obvious answer?

"What?"

"It leaves me time to work. To put into the company. Instead of her."

Joe tapped Cole on the head. "Ding, ding, ding. I think he finally got it."

"What's wrong with being successful, though? Isn't that the American dream?"

"Hell, yes, it is. But what's the good of all that success if you end up a sad old man sitting in a dark room, all alone at the end of your life?"

Cole chuckled. "Gee, thanks for the bright picture of my future." He said the words like a joke, but even he could see it ending up that way. He'd invest all his energy in the company, and then end up alone, because he'd forgotten to save some of that energy for the people in his life.

"So what are you going to do about it?" Joe asked.

"Get back to work," Cole said, getting to his feet and leaving the beer on the stoop. "That's the only answer I know."

He picked up the ax and went back to chopping wood. As the metal blade hit log after log, slivering them into fireplace-sized chunks,

Cole told himself he was making progress, when he knew damned well he wasn't doing much more than staying in place.

"You can do this," Emily muttered to herself and faced the daunting task assembled before her on the kitchen counter. Carol had gone into town for the day, off on a hair and manicure day arranged by Emily, who'd figured the stressed inn owner could use a little R & R. Martin Johnson, who'd been around the inn often to help Cole with some of the repair projects, had asked Carol if she might want to meet for lunch. Carol had fretted for an hour over her outfit for the day, changing three times before she left.

While Carol was gone, Emily promised to make dinner for everyone. She had to learn how to cook sometime. Better to start now and get some kind of kitchen skills under her belt before the baby came, or Emily would be weaning Sweet Pea on General Tso's chicken and fried rice from Mr Chow.

"Can't have you eating takeout every day, can I, Sweet Pea?" she said to the tiny bump under her belly. "Okay, let's figure this out."

She braced her hands on the counter and read over the recipe again. Seemed simple enough. For someone who knew what they were doing. Outside, she heard the sound of two axes hitting logs over and over as Cole and Joe chopped wood for the fireplace at the inn. At the rate they were going, Carol would be well stocked into next winter.

Joe had come into the kitchen earlier for some lunch, and spent some time catching up with Emily, telling her that Cole had asked him to help out with the repairs. She was glad. Not just because Cole needed the help, but because it was nice to see Cole's friend, and to hear about his life for the past few years.

Except every time she looked at Cole and Joe together, it was like her wedding day all over again. She was walking down the aisle toward a nervous Cole flanked by a grinning Turner, then backed up by Joe, who'd been smiling through his hangover. Emily remembered the excitement, the rush of joy, the hopes and dreams she'd had that afternoon, when Cole had lifted her veil and kissed her. It had been a simple, small wedding on a limited budget, but perfect.

Thinking about the wedding made her melancholy and nostalgic. Not a good strategy right now, because it muddied the very waters she had come here to clear. So she'd make a chicken potpie and let the task take her mind in a different direction.

She reached for the onion, celery and carrots and placed them on the cutting board, then picked up the chef's knife. She grabbed the onion first and raised the blade.

"I wouldn't do that if I were you."

She looked up to find Cole standing in the back door. Damn. How did the man always manage to look so handsome? He had on a thick dark green sweatshirt, dark jeans and new work boots. His hair was getting a little long, she noticed, but it only added to his sex appeal. "Do what?"

"Cut the onion first. Leave that for last. That way, you aren't crying over your carrots. Or—" he took a step inside "—you could wait for me to wash up and I can help you."

"You? Help me. Cook." She scoffed. "Right. What have you ever cooked?"

"I'll have you know reheating takeout takes real skill." He grinned, then crossed to the sink, pushed up his sleeves and scrubbed his hands. When he was done, he grabbed a second cutting board and knife and set them up across from Emily. "Two terrible cooks in the kitchen has to be better than one, don't you think?"

She laughed. "It could be double the disaster."

Cole leaned over the bar and lowered his voice. "Then blame it all on me and call for pizza."

The temptation to have him here, in the close quarters of the kitchen, rolled over her. Every nerve in her body was tuned to his presence, even when he was outside working. She'd glanced out the window a hundred times already this morning, catching quick glimpses of him replacing some of the siding. He surely had a long list of outdoor activities to complete, yet he wanted to be here, to help her make a chicken potpie. Nothing else. Right?

"Deal." She turned the cookbook toward him. "We're making chicken potpie."

Cole skimmed the directions. "I'm good with the chicken and vegetables part, but I have to admit, the words roux and piecrust have me terrified. What the hell is a roux?"

She laughed. "I have no idea."

Cole read over the directions again. "Sure you don't want to just call for pizza?"

"Cole Watson, you're not giving up already, are you?"

"Me? Never."

"Me, either." She turned the book back toward herself. "Besides, I need to learn how to do this."

"Why? Why now?"

"Because it's about darn time I learned how to cook," she said, instead of the truth—that she had this dream of baking cookies with her child. Of being in the kitchen with Sweet Pea on a stool, helping to measure and stir. Building a family life of just two. She'd wanted that for so long—

Then why did the thought suddenly sadden her?

Outside, she could hear the sound of Joe chopping wood. She gestured toward the door. "If you want to help Joe, I can handle this."

Cole arched a brow.

"I can figure it out. And if I don't, I'll blame you and call for pizza." She grinned, half hoping he'd leave, half hoping he'd stay.

"I'd rather stay and help you. I should learn to cook, too, since I'm living on my own now."

She didn't remind him that he could afford a team of chefs to make him food around the clock.

"After all," Cole said, leaning in toward her again, "didn't you say you always wanted me to help you instead of hiring someone to do the work? Let me help you, Emily."

She considered him for a moment. What would it hurt? Maybe together they could puzzle through this whole roux and piecrust thing. He had a point. She couldn't say no when he was offering the very thing she'd asked him for.

"Okay, then, you have onion duty." She plopped the offending vegetable onto Cole's cutting board.

"You just want to see me cry."

"No, but it is definitely a bonus." She took the celery, trimmed off the ends and began to cut it into little green crescent shapes. Across from her, Cole had peeled the onion and sliced it down the middle. He made slow, neat, precise slices in the vegetable, so exact it was as if he'd measured them.

Cole stopped cutting and looked up at her. "What?"

"You're treating that onion like it's a prototype or a stock report. It won't break if you chop it fast, Cole. We only have so long to get dinner on the table."

"I like things neat," he said.

"Neat? That's an understatement. You should have been an accountant, Cole, with all those straight lines. Though, there were a couple times you didn't mind a mess. One in particular I remember." The last few words came out as a whisper. "Remember the closet in our first apartment?"

"That wasn't a closet—it was an overgrown shoe box. It was impossible to keep neat." He stopped slicing and looked up at her, and a knowing smile curved across his face. The kind of smile that came with a shared history, a decade of memories. It was a nice, comfortable place to be.

"The ties," Cole said. "You're talking about the ties."

Oh, how she would miss this when her marriage was dissolved. All the memories they held together would be divided, like the furniture and the dishes and the books on the shelves. She'd be starting over with someone else. A blank slate, with no inside jokes about food fights and messy closets.

Emily craved those memories right now, craved the closeness they inspired. Just a little more, she told herself, and then she'd be ready to let go. "Remember that day you couldn't find the red one with the white stripes?"

He nodded. "The one you gave me for our first Christmas. I said it was my lucky tie and I wanted to wear it on my first sales call."

Their gazes met, the connection knitting

tighter. She smiled. "You were so mad, because you like everything all ordered, and this was out of order. So I tore the closet apart looking for it, and because I was frustrated and in a hurry, I just threw all the ties in a pile on the floor. You came in and found me—"

"And at first I was upset at the mess, but then you held up the tie—"

"And I told you that if you made a mess once in a while, maybe you wouldn't be so uptight."

They laughed, the merry sound ringing in the bright and cheery kitchen. "But you forget the best part," Cole said, moving a little closer, his voice darkening with desire. "How we ended up making love on that floor, on top of the ties, and having a hell of a good time."

"In the middle of a mess."

It had been a wild, uninhibited moment. They'd had so few of those. Too few.

Cole caught a strand of her hair in his fingers and let the slippery tress slide away. "Why didn't I do that more often, Emily?"

She ached to lean into his touch, to turn her lips to his palm, to kiss the hand she knew so well. "I don't know, Cole, I really don't."

He held her gaze for a moment, then a mischievous light appeared in his eyes and his hand dropped away. He shifted his attention to the onion again, and this time did a frantic chopping, sending pieces here and there, mincing it into a variety of tiny cubes. "There. Done. And messy as hell."

She laughed. "I think the pie will be all the better for it."

"Oh, yeah? Wait till we make the crust. You might not feel that way with flour in your hair."

"You wouldn't."

He eyed the five-pound bag of all-purpose flour on the counter. "Oh, I would. And I will. I never did get you back for throwing my ties on the floor." Cole came around to the other side of the bar, scooping up a bit of flour in his hand. "Are you sorry about that?" he asked.

There was a charge in the air, fueled by the innuendos and heat between them. It was delicious and sweet and she hoped the feeling stayed. "Not one bit."

Cole held his hand over her head. "You want to rethink your position, Mrs. Watson?"

She hadn't been called that in months, and the name jarred her for a second. She remembered when Cole had first proposed and she had written *Mrs. Cole Watson* a hundred times, until the proposal felt real and she could believe she was really going to marry the man of her dreams. Soon, she wouldn't be Mrs. Watson anymore. Or a missus at all.

"I'm sorry, Cole," she said softly.

He dropped his hand and met her gaze. "They were just ties, Emily. I didn't really care."

"I know," she said. She was trying to hold on to the moment, but knew it was a butterfly, fleeting, impossible to catch. Eventually, Cole would go back to work, and she'd be on her own again. A single mom. Better to end it now than to prolong the inevitable. Emily returned to the vegetables. "Let's, uh, get this pie made before Carol comes home."

If he sensed the change in her, he didn't say anything. He helped her finish chopping the vegetables and cooked chicken, then lifted the heavy food processor onto the counter and helped her assemble the ingredients for the piecrust. "Okay. Here goes nothing," Cole said, pushing the pulse button. Several pulses later, the flour and butter and ice water had coalesced into a crust. "Voilà!" Cole said, lifting off the plastic lid. "Piecrust."

"I am impressed," she said. "What are you doing for your next trick, Superman?"

He grinned. "That you will have to wait to see, Mrs. Watson."

She shook her head and dipped her gaze before he saw the tears that had rushed to her eyes. "Don't call me that, Cole. Please."

"Emily, Emily," he said, tipping her chin until she was looking at him. "We cleaned up the mess with the ties. Why do you have such little faith that we can clean up the mess with our marriage?"

CHAPTER NINE

THE FOUR OF them sat around the long dining room table, helping themselves to big slices of chicken potpie and generous bowls of tossed salad. Carol had brought home a loaf of bread from the bakery in town, which served as the perfect complement to the meal. Cole sat beside Joe, across from Emily and Carol in a warm and cozy room filled with great scents, great food and great people.

This, he thought, *this is what home feels like.*

Was that what he and Emily had missed? Had they been so fixated on getting from A to B that they had missed that critical step of building a home, not just a house?

Or rather, had he? Emily had asked him to be home more often, and he'd promised over and over to do that, only to spend his time at work instead. Then they'd built that house on the hill, and despite the fact that it had a table in the kitchen, a handcrafted one in the dining room and another outdoor eating space, they rarely ate together. Most nights, she had been asleep before he got home, and then he was gone again before she was awake.

"Great job, Emily." Carol gestured toward the chicken potpie. "Maybe I should hire you on as a chef."

Emily laughed. Cole liked it when she laughed, because her face and eyes lit up, and the whole room felt lighter. "I am far from being a chef. Cole's the one who mastered the piecrust. I just read the directions."

"You did more than that, Emily," Cole said. "You taught me how to chop an onion, too."

She dipped her head, a flush shading her cheeks. "I just told you it didn't have to be all perfect."

Joe looked from Cole to Emily and back again. "You got this guy to loosen the reins a little? What'd you do, drug him?"

"Hey, I'm not that bad," Cole said.

"*Right*. You are the only man I know who had a typewritten itinerary for your own bachelor party." Joe chuckled.

Cole scowled. "I like to be organized. So sue me."

Joe leaned toward Emily with a conspiratorial grin. He cupped his hand around his mouth, mocking a whisper. "If you want to drive Cole crazy, just hide his lists and his planners."

"First I'd have to pry his smartphone out of his hands," Emily said, laughter in her voice. "And that's almost impossible."

Cole unclipped the phone and slid it across the table toward Emily. "Hey, I can disconnect the umbilical."

Joe scoffed. "That's not a challenge. It's already after five."

The cell phone sat on the table, one of the things that had built his company to its current position at the top, but also one of the things that had dragged his marriage to the bottom. That was one of the hazards of always being available—it was good for business, but bad for a relationship.

Emily glanced at his phone, then slid it back. "I don't need it. I'm just glad you're getting some time away from the office here."

"Are you glad I'm here?" he asked, his gaze meeting hers.

A small, bittersweet smile crossed her lips. "Of course. You work so hard, I was always worried you'd have a heart attack. You need some time to destress."

That wasn't what Cole had hoped Emily would say. He'd wanted her to say she was glad he was here with her, finally trying to work on their marriage again.

"And in the process," Emily added, "maybe you can get back to what's important."

The last few words had him trying to read Em's face, but her gaze was on her plate, keeping whatever secrets she had hidden behind her wide green eyes.

"That's what this inn was always about. Helping people get in touch with their lives, themselves," Carol said. "And what I'd like to do more of if I end up keeping it. I think it'd make a great retreat for corporate types who want to get out from behind the desk."

"You could make it a win-win," Joe said with a grin. "Give them some hammers and nails or some paint and a paintbrush and put them to work on that project list that Cole drew up. You'll get the stuff done around here, and they'll get to do something other than sit around an office all day. Plus, Cole would get to check things off on one of his lists, and we all know how happy that makes him."

Cole laughed. Damn, it was good to have

Joe here. His friend kept him grounded, real. "Joe, only you would make people work on vacation."

Emily dished up some more salad and grabbed another slice of bread. "Says the man who hasn't taken a vacation in years."

"True." Cole gave her a nod, then leaned in with a grin. "Maybe you should have kidnapped me and whisked me away to an undisclosed location. Out of network range, of course."

A mischievous glint shone in her eyes. "That might have been fun."

"Just for the record, if you ever get the urge to do something like that, I'm game." It seemed as if the room had closed to just the two of them. He held her gaze, and his heart skipped a beat. "But you might want to take my phone first."

"If I get that thing in my hands, I'll end up smashing it with a sledgehammer," Emily said with a teasing smile. "It's needier than a three-year-old."

As if on cue, the smartphone began to ring and the caller ID screen lit. Doug, probably calling about another problem with the new product launch. Cole reached forward, pressed the button on the side of the phone, sent the call to voice mail and darkened the screen. The action sent a flicker of anxiety through him, but he pushed it aside. Emily was right. He'd spent far too much time letting work interrupt dinners, and the last thing he wanted was an interruption in this one, when things seemed to be going so well, almost like the old days.

"That's a good start," Emily said, and gave him a smile that he wanted to hold in his heart. "Thank you, Cole."

The dinner ended too soon. Carol began to pick up the dishes and put out a hand to stop Cole and Emily when they rose to help her. "You two go off on a walk or something. Joe and I can get these."

"Are you sure?" Emily asked. "You already do so much."

"That's my job. Your job is to go relax," Carol said. "And that's an order."

"Don't worry about Carol," Joe said. He flexed his biceps. "She's got a whole lotta help."

Cole chuckled. "A whole lotta something, that's for sure." Then he turned to Emily, glad that Carol had made it impossible for Emily to say no. "Want to take a walk? It's not too cold out tonight."

She glanced at Carol, who nodded and waved her off. "Okay. Let me get my coat."

A few minutes later, they were outside, breathing in the crisp fall night air. The scent of a wood-burning stove filled the air, mixing in the fragrance of cedar and oak. "It's a beautiful night," Cole said. "Look at the lake. It's as smooth as glass."

"It's gorgeous. Like a postcard." Her breath frosted in the air, surrounding her face with a soft cloud.

He thought of what she had said before, about how he should learn to make a mess more often, to be less uptight and rigid and planned. Spontaneity had never been Cole's strong suit, yet the happiest times he could remember were when he went off schedule. Maybe that was the key to finding his way back to where they used to be—throwing out the plan and just…

Being.

A rowboat lay on the beach, flanked by a pair of oars. The moon glinted off the wooden boat's hull, making it look like a giant smile in the dark. "Hey, let's take the boat out," he said.

"At night? In the middle of November?"

He leaned in close, catching the sweet scent of her floral perfume, a fragrance he knew as well as he knew his own name. Her hair drifted across his lips. "Live on the edge, Emily," he whispered. "With me."

She turned to him, her lips an inch away from his. Her eyes widened, she inhaled, and Cole wanted her more in that moment than he could remember. "On the edge? But it's dangerous. It's nighttime, the water is cold and… well, things could go wrong. Remember the story Carol told?"

He brushed the hair off her forehead and let his touch linger there a moment. "Don't worry. I'll be there to catch you." His hand drifted down, along her jaw. "I always will be."

She shook her head, and tears glimmered in her eyes. "Cole—"

"Trust me, Em. Just tonight."

She bit her lip and watched him for a moment, wary, hesitant.

"It'll be fun. Unscripted, spontaneous, fun. I promise."

Then the hesitation disappeared and she smiled. "Okay. As long as you don't rock the boat."

He took her hand and led her down the hill. Her hand felt good in his, right. Long ago, they had stopped holding hands. Why, he couldn't remember. If they ever got back together, he vowed that if Emily was nearby, he would always hold her hand. "Of course. Not rocking the boat is my specialty."

"You're wrong about that, Cole. *I'm* the one who never likes to rock the boat," she said, bending to help him right the boat and slide it into the water. "You're the one who takes chances."

"In business, yes. In my personal life—" he took an oar, then waited while she climbed into the rowboat before handing her the second oar "—not so much."

Cole gave the boat a push, and it slid into the water with a gentle ripple. He took both of the oars, positioned himself on the bench, then began rowing away from the shore. The oars made a satisfying whoosh sound with each stroke, while his back and shoulder muscles jerked to attention. A fish jumped out of the water behind them, then flopped back in, spattering them. Emily watched him row, a smile playing on her lips. "What?" he asked.

"You look...well, you look sexy and strong doing that."

"Then maybe I should do this more often."

She didn't respond to that, just smiled again and leaned back on the bench. "All the times I've been to the Gingerbread Inn, I've never been out on the lake after dark. It's so peaceful out here."

A perfect setting for a man to propose, Cole thought. When he'd proposed to Emily all those years ago, he'd done what he always did—he'd created a plan for the evening and stuck to his timetable, almost to the minute. Dinner in the city, followed by the ubiquitous and clichéd carriage ride along New York's streets, then pausing by Central Park to slip onto the carriage's carpeted floor and pop the question. He'd known Em was going to say yes before he even asked, because they'd talked about getting married a half dozen times before.

Out here, alone in the dark while fish bobbed in the water around them and geese swam silently along the banks, he had the perfect setting for something unexpected. Something that would show Emily he wasn't here to fix the porch or chop firewood. He was here for them. For a second chance. He gave the oars a final tug, then set them across the center of the boat. Then he leaned forward, dropping to one knee, and reached for his wife's hands.

"What are you doing?" she asked.

"Living on the edge," he said. "Emily, I don't want a divorce. I don't want us to live apart anymore. I want to try again, to give our marriage the chance it needs. Will you try again?"

Her eyes widened, and she backed up a bit. Damn. This was why he planned these things out. So he could have time to write a good proposal, to plan out what he was going to say. That had to rank up there with the top ten least romantic proposals in the history of time. "Cole, there's a lot we need to discuss. Things we haven't settled yet."

"What's to settle? I love you." He held her hands, but noticed she didn't hold his back. Nor did she tell him she loved him. Had her feelings for him changed? Was he reading her all wrong?

"It's about more than love, Cole. It always was. We're...not on the same path anymore."

He grinned. Okay, so she hadn't said she didn't love him, either. He'd take that as a good sign. "We are now. A path that's kind of going in circles in the middle of the lake."

She pulled her hands back and tucked them inside her coat. The air between them dropped a few degrees, and the grin faded from Cole's face.

"I want a family, Cole. I always have. We've put it off forever, and honestly, it's gotten to the point where I don't understand why. You've achieved what you want with the company, I'm writing my book...what more is there to do or get before we have kids?"

Just the word *kids* made him freeze. When he'd first married Em, he'd told her he wanted children, and maybe for a time, he had. But as the years had worn on and he watched his friends have kids and have trouble and turmoil in their families, trouble and turmoil that affected the kids and ruined their childhoods, the more Cole didn't want to change the status quo. But he knew that telling Em would drive her away for good. She had always been set on having children, the one risk Cole didn't want to take. "We always wanted to travel, Em. Have fun, live our lives, before we added kids into the mix."

She let out a gust. "Let's go back to shore. This isn't getting us anywhere."

"Let me ask you this." He leaned toward her, causing the boat to make a gentle rocking motion. "Why do you think having kids will improve our lives?"

"How can you say they won't?" She shook her head. "I don't get you, Cole, I really don't."

"I'm just trying to make sure we have everything in order first." He didn't want to tell her that the thought of being a father was the only thing that truly scared Cole. He knew what he was good at and what he wasn't—and parenting didn't make the list of talents.

"You and your lists and timetables." She let out a gust. "For once, I wish you would just let all that go."

He was losing her. He could hear it in her voice, see it in her face. They had reached a moment of no return, a time when he had to act, instead of just talk. Their relationship stood on a fault line, and only a dramatic shift would keep it from falling apart.

"I can, if you want me to, Em." He tugged his cell out of his pocket and held it over the water. "I can drop this in the water, and not think twice about it. Devote myself entirely to us for the next week or month or year or however long it takes."

"You'd do that? Walk away from the company?"

"If it brings us back together, yes." Then, as if God was testing his resolve, Cole's phone began to ring. Doug, again. The little notification bar under the caller ID showed Doug had called four times with no answer. Definitely an emergency, if he was trying that hard to get hold of Cole.

He glanced at the screen, his stomach churning. The urge to answer the call, to solve the problem, burned inside him. The company had taken so much of his life in the past ten years and even now, even when it mattered, he couldn't let it go. He could feel the need calling to him, like the business held an invisible string to his gut. He wasn't sure which direction the need went—whether it was the company that needed him or him who needed the company. The phone dangled from his fingers, inches from the water. Then his fingers tightened their grip and the decision was made. He realized that at the same time Em did.

Emily gave him a sad little smile. "You might as well answer it."

"What about us?"

"Us?" She took the oars and put them in the water, then began rowing back toward shore. "The only thing I know for sure is that I'm done going in circles."

CHAPTER TEN

COLE CAUGHT UP to her after the boat was back on shore and Emily was already striding up the hill. "Where are you going?" he asked.

"Back inside." Where she belonged. Where she wouldn't have to think about that little rise of hope she'd had a few minutes ago when Cole had offered to throw his phone away—and answered it instead. She should have known better. He was doing what he'd always done—making promises that would dissolve as soon as they got back to real life.

"I thought we were talking."

She spun around. "I am tired of talking, Cole. We've done nothing but that for years. And where did it get us? Nowhere but divorced."

"We're not divorced yet, Emily. There's still—"

"I don't want to hear one more second about how there's still a chance. How many times did I say that to you? How many times did I try to make this work? Try to change our lives? And what did you do?" She cursed under her breath and shook her head, hating the pain in her chest, the tears burning the back of her eyes. God, why did this hurt so much? When would Cole stop having a hold on her heart? She wanted to scream at him, to tell him to stop putting her through this emotional roller coaster. The same one she'd ridden so many times in the past ten years, she could predict the next loop. There'd be a high, a wonderful honeymoon period of flowers and dinners out, followed on its heels by the plummeting lows of Cole's absence, an empty house and an empty bed. "You made a bunch of promises and then went to work. Which is what you're going to do this time, too, Cole. I know you. That is the curse of being married to you for so long. I know what you're going to do, and I keep coming back even though I know it's going to hurt."

"The company—"

"Was always number one. And I was somewhere in distant second place." She refused to cry. To let that hurt any more than it already had. But it did, oh, how it seared against her heart, the truth a branding iron that left a jagged scar.

Silence stretched between them for a long moment. "I never meant for that to happen."

"Yet it did, Cole. Do you know how many times I hoped and prayed and believed, and then you'd break my heart again?" She pressed a hand to her chest and forced herself to take a breath, to be strong, to sever this connection once and for all. "I can't do that anymore. I don't have it in me to go through that pain one more time. *Not one more time.*"

Emily had finally reached her breaking point. Maybe it was the baby, maybe it was being here at the inn, where she had first learned to believe in happy endings. Maybe it was that damned hope that had sprung up inside her when Cole arrived here, and when he stayed, and when he held his phone over the lake.

"The definition of insanity is doing the same thing over and over again and expecting a different result," she said, as much to herself as to him. "I'm *done* with this insanity, Cole."

The statement exited her with a measure of frustration and relief.

Done.

All this time, she'd never used the word *done*. She'd always believed there was a chance, but when he'd answered his phone on the lake, she'd known the truth. He was always going to go back to the way he was, and she was always going to be the one in second place.

"I'm done, Cole," she said again, softer this time.

"What if I'm not? What if I want to keep fighting for us?"

She shook her head, and braced her heart against the hope trying to worm its way back in there. "Where was all that six years ago, Cole? Or hell, six months ago? Now you show up, when it's over, when we're a few pieces of paper away from divorced, and you want me to believe you?"

"I have tried, too, Emily. I have tried to connect with you, tried to make this work. It's not just about the company taking too much of my time. You…" He shook his head. "You stopped giving time."

She opened her mouth to protest, then shut it again. He was right. There'd been dinners she had turned down, lunch dates she had skipped out on, late-night talks she had avoided. Cole would come and go in bursts of trying to fix them, then burying himself in work, and after a while, she learned to maintain her distance rather than trust. "It was too risky."

"Because when it didn't work out, you got hurt. Yeah, well, you weren't the only one."

In those vulnerable words, Emily heard pain, frustration, loss. An echo of what brimmed in her. They'd hurt each other, time and time again. The only thing to do, the only smart course to take, was to end this and stop the hurt, on both sides.

She nodded. "Cole, I can't do this anymore. I mean it. I'm—" she stopped before she said she was pregnant, and trying to conserve her energy, her heart, for the baby "—done."

Maybe if she said it enough, she would stick to that resolve. And Cole would believe her.

He eyed her, then, after a moment, nodded and let out a gust. "Then I guess my being here is a waste of my time."

A waste of his time. That hurt. What did she expect? That he would keep fighting and fighting for their marriage, showing her finally that he was committed? Yeah, maybe she had. And now, after just a few days, Cole was giving up.

"Maybe it is," she said, though the words hurt her throat and cost her something deep inside. She told herself it was better this way, better to let go now than to keep hoping. Sweet

Pea needed a dad to depend on, not one who came and went like the wind.

The next day, Emily fiddled with her book for a couple hours but didn't get much accomplished. The words that had flowed so easily earlier now refused to come. Probably because her mind was filled with images of Cole.

She was done, she reminded herself. Done, done, done.

He'd surprised her last night, not just with the excursion on the lake, but with the impromptu proposal. How she'd wanted to say yes, to believe that the Cole she'd seen in the past few days, the relaxed, easy man who had fallen asleep in the sun, would be the one she'd wake up next to tomorrow and every day after that.

But he wasn't, nor did he want the same future she did. Ending it now would save her a lot of heartache down the road. Even if it felt the opposite in the light of day.

Emily gave up on writing, tugged on a thick sweatshirt, then headed outside. There was a nip in the air, a definite sign that the pretty fall days were coming to an end.

That meant she also had to start thinking about where she was going to go. She couldn't stay here forever, though a part of her finally felt grounded here in this tiny town in Massachusetts, more familiar than the neighborhood where she'd lived with Cole for all those years. Maybe she'd rent a little house in town, settle down here and build a life with Sweet Pea. It would be a simple, uncomplicated life.

Yet the thought also saddened her. Cole didn't want children, and once they were divorced, she doubted he'd have much to do with their baby. After their cooking fun in the kitchen, she'd hoped that maybe things would be different, but it was clear the same walls stood between them now as always. With Cole, the company came first, and family came in a distant second, if at all. She'd be raising this child on her own, and in the end, Cole would be the loser.

Cole's rental wasn't in the drive, but Martin Johnson's van was, which explained why Carol had been busy fixing her hair when Emily told her she was going for a walk. Emily smiled. The inn owner was a nice woman and deserved a man who would treat her well.

"Hey, Emily," Joe said when she stepped outside. He had a window propped on a sawhorse, removing the old glaze in order to fix a broken pane. "Cole went into town for some supplies. He should be back soon."

"That's okay. I'm not looking for Cole."

Joe leaned the window against the sawhorse and crossed to Emily. "I hate seeing you guys like this. Cole's miserable...you're miserable. Are you sure you can't work it out?"

"I wish we could, I really do. But it's over." She let out a long breath. "I still love him. Heck, I probably always will. But we just want different things out of life."

Joe flashed her a grin. "It seemed like you were on the right track last night at dinner."

"I thought so, too. And in a lot of ways, we are. But not in the most important ways, so I told him last night that I'm done for good." Emily tucked her hair behind her ears. It didn't seem right to feel this sad on such a pretty day. She had something wonderful to look forward to, and she needed to focus on that, not the problems that would soon be in her past. "I'm just tired of waiting for him to be ready to start a family and to put family first."

"Ah, that explains a lot." Joe grabbed a water bottle out of the cooler at his feet and took a long sip. "Did Cole say why he doesn't want to have kids?"

"He keeps saying we haven't done this or

that. Traveled enough. Been together long enough." She exhaled. "If you ask me, they're all excuses."

"If you ask me, I think you're right." Joe tipped the bottle in her direction and arched a brow. "The question is why a smart man like Cole would make excuses like that."

Emily threw up her hands. "I don't know."

Joe nodded. His gaze went off to the distance for a moment as if he was trying to decide whether to say the next words. Finally, he returned his attention to Emily. "Did you ever meet Cole's parents?"

"Once. A long time ago, while we were still dating. Then his dad died and his mom moved to Arizona, and... Gosh, I can't believe it's been that long since we've seen his mom." She didn't have the best relationship with her parents, but at least she saw them for holidays and talked to them once a week. Cole, however, didn't call very often and had never wanted to go to Arizona. Yet another aspect of family he kept down the list from his hours at work. That alone should have told her where their child would rank.

"I've known Cole a long, long time," Joe said. "And I knew his parents, too. Let's just say he didn't have the ideal childhood."

"He never talks about it." There were a few conversational topics that Cole steered away from. His childhood was one of them. She'd sensed it hadn't been happy, something she could relate to, and had never pushed him to open up. Had she been avoiding the conversations that would have brought them closer? Had her efforts to keep the peace been part of the problem? "What happened?"

"His father was a tyrant, to put it mildly. Nothing Cole ever did was good enough. Probably why he keeps on trying to be better, even when he's already the best in his industry. And his mother, well, she buried her head in a bottle and ignored everything around her." Joe shook his head. "Cole pretty much raised himself and his little brother. He told me a hundred times that he never wanted to have kids and treat them like that."

"But he's not like either one of them. Why is he still afraid of repeating their mistakes?"

Joe shrugged. "You'd have to ask him."

"Maybe." Emily started to head away. She didn't remind Joe that with the divorce looming, there'd be no conversations with Cole about his past. Done meant done, and she had to move on before she let herself get suckered back into riding that emotional roller coaster.

"Emily?" Joe said. She pivoted back. "Cole might not be the best at showing how he feels, or hell, even saying it, but believe me, that man loves you more than anything in the world. Keep an open heart."

That man loves you more than anything in the world. How she wanted to believe that. But she thought of him answering the phone last night, and knew there were things Cole loved more than her. And always would. "I thought the expression was keep an open mind."

"When it comes to Cole, an open heart's a better idea." Joe gave her a grin, then got back to work on the window.

Emily nodded, not making any promises, then strode down the dock, sat on the end and let her feet dangle above the deep blue water. The breeze skipped across the water, making it look like corrugated denim. Beautiful, serene.

She fingered the rock in her pocket and thought back to the day the four of them had found the rocks, scattered at the edge of the lake. The stones were so similar that the girls had taken it as a sign that they needed to keep them and make them special. So they'd stood by the water, holding hands and promising to always follow their dreams.

It had taken Emily a while, but she was

doing that now. She wondered if Andrea and Casey were doing the same thing, or if they were stuck in Neutral like Emily had been for far too long. Oh, how she missed the other Gingerbread Girls. Maybe a talk with her friends would take her mind off Cole, and all that Joe had said.

Emily tugged out her cell, then dialed Andrea. When her old friend answered, nostalgia filled Emily's heart. She could think of no one better to share this moment with than one of the other Gingerbread Girls. "Guess where I am?"

Andrea paused a moment, thinking. "On the end of the dock, watching for the Loch Ness monster to show up."

Emily laughed. "Guilty as charged. I can't believe we thought Nessie could really be here."

"Didn't keep us from swimming. Heck, our parents had to drag us out of the water most days."

So many memories, wrapped up in this magical place and those endless summers they had spent here. Such a blessing that their parents had loved this place just as much, bringing the families together summer after summer. The Gingerbread Girls had bonded, and been off all day, swimming, playing badminton, chasing boys...just being young and free. "We did have a lot of fun here."

"My best memories are all in that place." Andrea sighed. "Is Carol still planning on selling?"

Emily hadn't brought up the subject with Carol because she didn't want to hear the answer. She hoped that once the building was fixed, the innkeeper would change her mind. "I'm not sure. Cole has been doing a lot of repairs—"

"He's still there?"

Emily tossed a leaf into the water and watched it float away. "He wants a second chance. He keeps telling me things will be different."

"Maybe they will. Maybe the separation really changed him. I mean, he's still there, not at work, right? For a workaholic to take that much time off must mean something. Don't you think?"

Emily wanted to believe that, but she'd had her hopes dashed a thousand times before. And now, with the baby on the way, and Cole's insistence that they not add kids into their marriage, she didn't see a way to make it work, regardless of how many hours he spent here.

Not to mention there were things about himself that he had shared with Joe and not with her. His wife. If anything told Emily that their relationship wasn't on solid ground, that did.

"The fundamental differences between us are still there, Andrea," she said. "Nothing has changed that. I told him I'm moving forward with the divorce."

"I'm sorry. I know that's got to be hard on you."

"I'm okay. One of the things I'm finding by being on my own is that I'm stronger than I thought." She watched a lone bird skim the surface of the water, elegant and clean, then make a sudden dive for a fish. "Plus, I'm finally writing that book I wanted to write, and being responsible for me and only me. So even if Cole wanted to get back together, I'm not the same Emily I was before."

"That's fabulous. And I'll get to see that for myself when I get out there in a couple weeks."

"You're coming? Oh, that's awesome! It'll be so great to see you."

Andrea sighed. "You were right—I do need a break—and what better place to take a break than at the inn with all of you? And maybe the two of us can convince Carol that she needs to hold on to that place."

Emily smiled. "She'd be powerless against the combined strength of the Gingerbread Girls."

"You know it. Together, we were an unstoppable force." Then Andrea's voice lowered almost to a whisper. "Even without Melissa."

"That's why I'm here," Emily said. "Because of her letter. I want to go after my dreams before it's too late."

"That's the right attitude. And I'll be right there with you, soon. Take care, Emily."

"I will. See you soon." She hung up the phone and leaned back to turn her face to the sun. The wind rustled in the trees, creaked with the swaying dock and ruffled her hair. She closed her eyes and just let the day wash over her.

"Maybe I should have built a lake at the house in New York. Added a dock, a little boat." Cole's voice, behind her.

One of these days her stubborn heart would stop leaping every time Cole was around. But that day wasn't today.

She thought about what Joe had said. Maybe there was more to the story, more to Cole than she realized. Maybe she should keep an open heart. For a little while longer.

"And if we had a lake at the house in New

York, would we go fishing at the end of the day?" she asked, turning toward him. "I can just see you out there in hip waders with a fly rod."

"What, you don't think I'd look sexy in hip waders?"

She laughed. Picturing Cole in the long boots, with his jeans and mussed longish hair sent a ribbon of heat through her. That resolve to be done, to distance herself from him, fizzled for a moment. "You…you would look sexy in anything. Except maybe hip waders."

"I could rock some hip waders. I'll have to get some just to prove it to you." He cocked a hip and struck a pose.

She laughed more, and realized how long it had been since she'd laughed about something silly with Cole. Those days had got lost in the stress of building a business, then the busyness of the social life expected of someone in the upper orbit of moneymakers. She glanced at Cole and saw the smile lighting his face, his eyes. No matter what happened in the future, she hoped he managed to find more time and room for laughter. "You've looked so relaxed these past few days, Cole. So…happy. I haven't seen you like that in a long time."

He gestured toward the space beside her.

Emily nodded, and Cole sat down on the dock's edge. "I didn't realize how much I was working until I wasn't there every day." He glanced over at her. "All those years you told me I needed to take a vacation, and I didn't. I guess I thought the place would fall apart if I wasn't there."

"And is it?"

He chuckled. "Probably. Given how many messages are on my phone, and how often people call me. Like last night. That was a problem with the shipping company that had Doug in a panic. I got it straightened out, then told Doug not to call me unless the building was on fire. I hired good people, and they'll figure those things out. That is, after all, what I pay them to do, as Irene and you have reminded me."

"They're probably all still in shock that you actually took several days off in a row."

He nodded, then picked up a stick from the dock and flung it into the water. "I should have done it years ago. Maybe then we wouldn't be where we are now."

"Maybe." She watched the stick float for a moment, then disappear beneath one of the ripples in the lake. "There was a lot more wrong in our marriage than the fact that we never went on vacations, you know."

"But if we had gone on vacation more often, then maybe we could have talked about those other things." He flung another stick out onto the water and waited until a wave devoured it. "That's why I'm not going back to work any-time soon. I'm staying until this place is fixed or—" he turned to face her "—until we are."

"Cole, I can't—"

He put up a finger, pressing it to her lips. She closed her eyes, inhaled his familiar co-logne, and with it, the desire for the man she had married. "Don't say that. I know you want to file. I know you're done. But I started some-thing here that I want to finish, and if we're going to be staying in the same place, all I ask is for a few more days. After ten years, a few days isn't much, Emily. Is it?"

She shivered as the wind kicked up, and tugged the zipper of her sweatshirt higher. "Then tell me the real reason you don't want to have kids, Cole."

He opened his mouth, closed it again. "I never said I didn't want to have kids, Emily. Just not now."

"Why?"

"I don't have a reason why. It's just not the right time."

Why wouldn't he open up to her? Tell her at

least what he had told Joe? She wanted to tell him she already knew, but didn't want to betray Joe's confidence, either. The urge to yell at Cole returned, but where had fighting ever got them? All that anger had created a wall, and people didn't communicate through walls. So she took a deep breath instead.

"When will be the right time?" she asked softly. "Because I'm ready now."

More ready than you know.

"I don't know." He waved his hand vaguely. "Down the road someday."

She got to her feet. If he wasn't going to be honest with her, then she was wasting her time hoping for a change. "Just go back to the office, Cole. Staying here and repairing the plumbing or fixing the porch isn't going to change anything between us."

"You don't know that, Emily. If we talk—"

"I came here to get away, Cole. To think, without you around. I don't want to talk anymore. I told you last night that I'm done." She threw up her hands. "Why can't you be done, too? Then we can move on. Both of us."

He scrambled to his feet before she could leave, and reached for her hands. When Cole touched her, the familiar zing of electricity ran through Emily. Would there ever be a day when that didn't happen? And why, oh why didn't her heart and body get the message from her brain?

"Fine. But before we leave this place and move on to lawyers and court dates and divorce papers, I want to ask you to give us one more chance."

"Cole—" She turned away.

He tipped her chin until she was looking at him again. "Give *me* one more chance at least. Give me the next few days, and let's see what happens. No talk of divorce or separation or anything other than just…getting to know each other again. Having those talks we never had."

She knew she should say no. She even opened her mouth to say the word, but it got stuck in her throat. Maybe Cole realized he needed to open up, too. If he did, then there was a chance they could make this work. A small chance. "And at the end of that time?"

"If we realize we are too far apart to put this back together, that there's really nothing there to keep us together, then I will go back to New York and file myself."

Maybe if she agreed, he'd finally quit fighting a battle he was never going to win. And maybe she would stop looking at him and longing for the man he used to be. She hesitated, her gaze going to the lake, now as serene as a mirror.

"Okay," she said, because that darn bubble of hope refused to die, no matter how much her common sense tried to overrule it, "we'll try it."

A smile winged across Cole's face, and Emily wondered if maybe she shouldn't have given him that hope. Maybe she should have just told him to forget it, that she was having a baby he'd made it clear he didn't want, and it was silly to delay the inevitable.

"Be ready at six," Cole said.

"Why?"

Cole caught her chin, let his thumb trace a light touch along her bottom lip. Her heart skipped; her breath caught. "I want to take my wife on a date. One that should bring back some memories. Or at the very least, give us some new ones to share."

He turned to walk away, and she thought how much she wanted those. Her hand drifted to her abdomen. Oh, yes, how very, very much.

CHAPTER ELEVEN

COLE HADN'T BEEN this nervous since he was fifteen and asking a girl on a date. The date had been a stumbling, embarrassing event, ending with him spilling popcorn on her at the movies. Back then, he'd thought the stakes could never get higher than asking one of the most popular girls in high school to a movie.

He'd been wrong. Tonight's date would set the tone for whatever came next. He knew that as well as he knew the sun would rise tomorrow. If tonight went badly, it would add another brick to the wall between them. Too many bricks, and he knew the wall would be impossible to tear down.

When he'd proposed the date, he'd started thinking about calling for a limo or a private plane, taking Emily off to an elaborate dinner in Manhattan or a weekend on one of the Virgin Islands. Then he thought about everything she had said and that they had talked about, and realized that in order to solve the problems in the present, he needed to go back to the past.

The problem was that Cole had worked very hard to leave his past in the rearview mirror. As soon as he could shed the things that had held him down, he'd breathe a sigh of relief. Emily had never understood why he didn't want to visit his mother. Why he rarely went back to his hometown.

He'd met her family, and though they were far from perfect, they were a sight better than his parents had been. How could he explain to Emily that he never talked about his childhood because all it did was remind him of the very place he never wanted to be again?

All these years, he'd kept that to himself. Maybe that had been a mistake. Either way, he was here tonight to try to make things better, no matter what that took.

At six on the dot, he strode up the new steps of the porch and pressed the inn's doorbell. He adjusted his tie, shifted from foot to foot on his shiny dress shoes. A second later, Emily opened the door and gave him a curious look. "You rang the doorbell?" she said.

"Yup. I'm here to take my wife on a date. I thought I should do it right."

A small smile curved across her face, and amusement danced in her eyes. Score one for Cole. "Well, then, maybe I should call my dad and have him come over and grill you."

Cole laughed. He put up his right hand. "I promise not to drive too fast, to drink or to take advantage of you tonight. And I will have you home by curfew."

The smile widened. She put out her arm and he slipped it into the crook of his. "Then let's go," she said.

"Your wish is my command, madam." He led her down the porch and over to his rental car, opening the passenger's side door of the Mercedes and waiting for her to sit before coming around to the driver's side.

"What, no limo?" she said when he got behind the wheel.

"I thought we'd do this old school. No limos, no helicopters. No red carpets. Just a good old-fashioned date." He rested his hand on the key fob, then looked over at her. "Like we used to have. Before…everything."

The smile lit her eyes. "That sounds perfect, Cole."

He put the car in gear. They swung out of

the inn's drive and headed down the tree-lined road. Night was beginning to fall, and the waning sun dropped a dark gold hue over the treetops and streets. The pavement gleamed from an afternoon shower, making wet leaves cling to the tar in clumps.

"Where are we going?" Emily asked.

He shifted his gaze to her. She'd worn a dress, a simple deep green one that hugged her curves and showed off her amazing legs. She'd paired the dress with black heels and a long black trench coat that he'd given her for Christmas three years ago. Her hair was up, and a few loose tendrils dusted her neck and jaw. All in all, the effect was...devastating. Half of him didn't want to take her anywhere but to bed. Then he remembered his promise not to take advantage. He redirected his attention to the road before his hormones overruled that decision. "It's going to be a surprise," he said, "but we aren't going far."

"No dinner in the city? Hmm...I'm intrigued."

"Good." He took a left, then a right, and after another mile, he pulled into a parking lot and turned off the car. A few other cars filled the lot, while a bright white sign above announced their destination.

Emily turned to him, her eyes bright and excited. "You brought me to the Barrow's Cove Diner? This was my favorite place to eat when we were here in the summers. My mom and dad would bring me here on Friday nights. It was the one night we all ate as a family."

Cole grinned. "I know. I remember you telling me about that. But we're not going there quite yet."

He got out of the car, came around, opened her door, then put out his arm. She slipped hers into his again, and when he covered her hand with his own, Cole realized how much he had missed the simple act of touching his wife. When had it become more usual for them not to touch, than to have contact?

"It's still light out. Let's go for a short walk before dinner."

"A pre-feast calorie burn?"

"Something like that." He took her hand with his, and though she tensed, she didn't pull away. Score another point for Cole. He liked to think he was making progress with Emily, but at the same time he sensed she was holding something back. "Remember that game we used to play when we were young and poor?"

"What game?"

"The one where we picked out a house on

the street and imagined what we would be doing if we lived inside there." He remembered those days, strolling down the streets of New York at the end of the day, the two of them dreaming and wishing. In those days, it had seemed as if anything was possible, if only they believed hard enough.

"Back when we thought we'd never live in anything bigger than a bread box." She laughed. "We've kind of moved past that, haven't we, Cole?"

"Humor me, Emily." He didn't want to talk about how they weren't living in that giant house together anymore, how they were probably going to sell it and move on to separate residences. For this night, he wanted to pretend it was the old days, when the only thing they could afford was dreams.

She put a finger to her lip and studied the houses on either side of the street. "That one," Emily said, pointing to a small dark blue Cape Cod–style house with white trim. "To me, that house spells traditions. If we lived there, I'd be in the kitchen, cooking dinner and wearing an apron over my dress—"

"And pearls, don't forget the pearls," Cole said.

"Those and high heels, of course. The house

would be perfectly organized and clean, and my cooking would be impeccable. Then you would come home from work—"

"Precisely at five."

"And kiss me on the cheek, then sit in the recliner, put your feet up and read the paper while I finish dinner."

"That sounds like a great plan to me."

She gave him a gentle slug. "Yeah, good for the guy. Not so good for the woman. So don't get your hopes up, buddy, because it's never happening. Besides, I still can't cook."

"You made a hell of a chicken potpie the other day."

"With your help." She gave him an appreciative nod.

"Well, if we lived there, I'd help you make chicken potpie, Em. As long as you wore high heels a lot."

She shook her head, dismissing his words with a smile and a laugh. "Your turn. Pick a house."

He gestured toward a boxy white Georgian-style house. "In that house, I live a life of leisure, playing video games all day and eating Cheetos."

"And who is funding this life of leisure?"

"My bestselling novelist wife. Her first

novel, *Falling in Love with a Gamer,* hits the top of the bestseller charts and makes us all wealthy beyond our dreams."

"Hey!" She gave him another light jab. "Why is it that all these scenarios have you with the easy life?"

He laughed. "Because I am naturally lazy."

"That is as far from the truth as you can get. You are one of the hardest-working men I have ever met, Cole."

They had reached the end of the street and pivoted to head back toward the diner. "But I thought you hated how many hours I worked."

"I do. I did. But I still admire you for putting in the hours to go after what you wanted. You kept going when other people would have given up. When it comes to business, Cole, you are like a pit bull."

The implication—that he hadn't been that way about their marriage. He saw that now, and prayed for the thousandth time that he wasn't too late. He couldn't read Emily, though, and that concerned him. He'd always thought he knew her better than he knew himself, but lately it was as if she had opened an ever-widening divide between the two of them, one he couldn't get across no matter how hard he tried. Was it because she'd grown so far apart from

him that he couldn't reach her? Or was he just
that out of tune with the woman he had married?

Too soon, they reached the glass doors of the
diner. As soon as they walked inside, Emily
was greeted by the diner's hostess, an older
woman named Alice, who remembered Emily
from years before. The two chatted, then Alice
led them over to the last booth in the back corner. "Enjoy your meal, kids," she said to Cole
and Emily.

Cole tugged a menu out of the holder behind the napkin dispenser and handed the plas-
tic-coated paper to Emily. "I recommend the
chef's special," he said. "Tonight, that's meat
loaf and mashed potatoes."

She laughed. "I see you got the best table,
too."

"It's the most private one they had. No musi-
cians, but I hear if we stay late enough, Donny
Greer will get drunk and start serenading the
patrons."

Emily sat back against the red vinyl booth
and studied him. "You really know an awful
lot about this town for only being here a few
days."

He shrugged. "It's a friendly place. You

can't leave the hardware store without a new best friend."

"That must drive you crazy," Emily said. "I know how you hate to waste time on small talk."

In a business situation he hated delaying a meeting or a decision with chitchat about sports teams or the weather. In the office, Cole cut to the chase, intent only on getting through this task and on to the next demand on his time.

Since he had arrived in Barrow's Cove, though, he had taken the time to slow down, talk with the locals, enjoy the sunshine and turning leaves. He'd had more conversations with Emily in the past few days than the two of them had had in years. No matter where things went from here, Cole would make time for more of these small, simple conversations. Especially with Emily.

"Actually, I kind of like it," Cole said. "It reminds me of our old neighborhood. Remember Mrs. Timmons?"

Their elderly downstairs neighbor in that first terrible apartment building had possessed a sixth sense that had brought her out of her rooms every time Cole or Emily came home.

She'd been an inquisitive woman, but in a grandmotherly way.

The memory lit Emily's eyes. "Oh, my goodness. Mrs. Timmons. A little too friendly sometimes. I think she looked at us as her surrogate kids. Gosh, she was always on our doorstep, making sure we were eating right and getting enough sleep."

"If I remember right," he said, lowering his voice and leaning closer, "we were a little too busy to do much of either. And those were details we never shared with Mrs. Timmons."

Emily's face flushed. She raised the menu, blushed some more when she realized it was upside-down, then hurried to right it. She kept her gaze on the typed pages. "Uh, what are you thinking about ordering?"

"Tonight, I want the biggest burger they make."

"Really? Mr. Healthy Eating is getting a burger?"

"I figure I've burned off a burger and then some, doing all that work on the inn. And there's just something about working in the sun all day that makes a man want some red meat and a beer."

She laughed. "Next you'll be driving a pickup and chewing tobacco."

"I don't think there's a chance of that anytime soon." He grinned.

She studied the menu a while longer, then put it to the side. "You know what? I think I'll have the same. I'm ravenous all of a sudden."

"All that writing working up an appetite?"

"Yeah." She said that too fast, and hoped he wouldn't notice.

The waitress came by, saving Emily from having to answer any other questions about her sudden appetite. They ordered two burgers with fries, with Cole opting for a beer and Emily sticking to ice water.

Cole didn't notice she stayed away from alcohol, nor had he noticed her daily breakfast of crackers, the only thing that helped abate her morning sickness. Maybe he was just being a stereotypical clueless male.

Either way, she couldn't keep this secret forever. Before she knew it, she'd be sporting a baby bump—and that would be something Cole would notice for sure.

When the waitress was gone, Cole reached into his pocket and pulled out a small paper bag. "I have something for you," Cole said, "I meant to wrap it, but…"

"For as long as I've known you, you've never wrapped a present." She shook her head, amusement in her features. "I don't think you even know where we keep the Scotch tape."

He thought a second. "Okay, you've got me there. Where do we keep the Scotch tape?"

"The end drawer in the kitchen. The scissors are in there too, by the way."

He nodded. "I'll remember that for next time. I promise."

She bit her lip, not wanting to spoil the date by reminding him that they were going to sell the house, divvy up their possessions, and then he would have his own place for Scotch tape, and she would have her own. Because a part of her didn't want to be reminded that soon, they'd be living separate lives. She touched the blank spot on her left hand, a reminder she no longer wore her ring. Cole, however, still wore his gold band. As far as she knew, he hadn't taken it off once in ten years.

Instead of the dose of reality, she said, "And the wrapping paper is in the hall closet."

He smiled. "I'll remember that, too, Em. Now, open your gift."

She opened the bag and peeked inside to find a thick leather-bound journal and a silver pen. She drew them out, admiring the weight and quality of the gifts. "They're...beautiful."

He gestured toward the book. "The journal was handmade by Beatrice Wickham. She lives on the other side of the lake and has a little corner in the hardware store where she sells her handmade creations. She remembered you and said this would be perfect for, and I quote, 'that little girl who was always writing those stories.'"

Emily ran her hand over the stitched cover. A long crimson ribbon hung from the inside of the book, just waiting to mark her place. Her heart softened at the thoughtfulness of the gift. It was simple and special, not just because it had been handmade by a local artisan, but because it had been crafted in the one place on earth that meant so much to Emily. The same place that had been instrumental in the new direction she was taking with her life. "It's beautiful, Cole." Though the adjective, even repeated a second time, seemed inadequate.

Cole nodded toward the book. "Open it up."

She did as he asked and found an inscription on the first page. Cole's familiar slanted handwriting, all angles and precision, like the man himself, filled the space.

Use this book and pen to write the stories in your heart. Let it take you from once upon a time to happily ever after. And maybe, in the process, you can find your own happily ever after, too.

He hadn't signed his name, or used the word *Love*. She wondered if it was because he didn't want to push her or because he no longer felt that way about her. Either way, the gift touched her.

Because Cole had listened.

For almost ten years, she'd complained that he didn't listen, didn't pay attention, didn't engage. Now he was asking her where they kept the tape and writing words that encouraged her to pursue her dreams. Why now? Why after she had decided the marriage was over, and had steeled herself to say goodbye?

She raised her gaze and cursed the tears brimming in her eyes. "Why didn't you ever do this before?"

He crossed his hands on the table and let out a long breath. "Because I didn't realize that helping me go after my dreams came at the cost of yours. For a long time, I've fooled myself into thinking that you were happy, that you wanted all the same things I did. But now I know you sacrificed your dreams for mine. I'm sorry it took me so long to figure that out."

"It's okay, Cole." She placed her palm on

top of the book and imagined the words that would fill it in the weeks ahead. She'd sit on the porch of the inn or on the dock and scribble her ideas and snippets of scenes. It was the perfect vehicle to inspire and encourage her writing. "Thank you very much."

The waitress returned with their drinks. Cole raised his glass toward hers. "To new beginnings."

"To new beginnings," she echoed, and clinked against his. If he only knew the new beginning growing inside her right now.

A part of her felt horrible for keeping the secret from him. He deserved to know about the baby, even if he didn't want it. And maybe if he saw how determined she was to move forward as a single mom, he'd give up this hope that she wanted to go back to the life they'd had before. It was past time to tell Cole about the baby.

"You have that look again," Cole said. "The furrowed brow. The worry in your eyes. What's up?"

That was the problem with being married to a man for ten years. He noticed when she wasn't acting like herself. She tried to work up the courage to tell him, then chickened out at the last second when she saw the waitress approaching with their burgers. "Why don't we talk about it after dinner?"

Cole agreed, and as they dived into the juicy burgers, they talked about everything and nothing. The kind of easygoing conversations they used to have back in their college days, mingled with a lot of laughs. Cole filled her in on some updates about some of the people she knew at the company, and she told him the latest gossip from the wives. They traded golf tips, reminisced about a favorite restaurant that had shut its doors, and in general, acted like an ordinary couple.

All the while, the specter of Emily's secret waited on the sidelines. Once she told him, it would change everything.

When they were done, Cole paid the waitress, adding a generous tip, then took Emily's hand as they left the diner. The move felt so natural, so right. She leaned against his arm as they stepped out into the chilly late-November night. Without a word, Cole released her, and instead drew her close, shielding Emily from the cold. She had missed the simple touches between a couple, the way Cole could read her mind and provide what she needed at the moment she needed it most. Yet another sign he was finally paying attention.

"That was nice," she said.

"Very nice." He pressed a gentle, easy kiss against her forehead, and Emily thought that she couldn't have imagined a more perfect night with her husband. The warm comfort of being with someone who knew her filled Emily, and she began to believe that maybe they could right this sinking ship after all.

The only shadow that lingered at the end of the night was the secret in her belly. She pressed a hand over her abdomen and sent up a silent prayer that maybe Cole would be as excited about their child as she was.

Cole opened the door for her and she slid into the warmth of the rental car. He held her hand the whole way back to the inn, glancing over at her from time to time, as if to make sure she was real. Unspoken tension filled the dark space of the car, the tension that came with knowing they were both going back to a place with beds, a married couple who hadn't been together in a long, long time. Every once in a while, Cole would squeeze her hand, telling her he knew the same thing.

This could end in a sweet, delicious way, with her in his arms, in his bed. Oh, how she wanted that. She'd tell him later, she decided.

After just a little more of this, a few more minutes in this perfect bubble.

They pulled into the driveway, and Cole turned off the car, then turned to Emily in the dark. "Let's have more nights like that. From here on out, at least once a week. I think we just forgot how to connect, Emily. If we can start connecting again, then maybe we can get back to where we were."

"Or get to where we are going."

He nodded, then reached up and cupped her jaw. She leaned into the touch, drifted a kiss across his palm.

"Wherever that is, I want to go with you." Cole closed the distance between them and kissed her, softly at first, then shifting to a harder, hungrier embrace. Desire slid through her like hot syrup on pancakes, pooling in her gut, overriding her common sense. She knew Cole's body, and oh, how he knew hers.

Hot need spiked inside her, for the way he could make her body sing, for the touch of his fingers inside her, his kisses running down her body, over her breasts. One kiss, one touch, and she could have that, just one more time. What would it hurt?

Before she could think twice, Emily surged into her husband, driven by a desire too long unmet. She tangled her fingers in Cole's hair, drawing him halfway across the car. He groaned and crushed her to him, one hand sneaking between them in a hot hurry, sliding under her blouse, tugging out of her jeans, and then his hand was on her skin, fingers slipping under the band of her bra, sliding up, over her breast, cupping it while his thumb traced a ravenous circle around her nipple.

She fumbled with the buttons on his shirt, trying to undo them while she arched against his touch, distracted by the magic Cole's fingers created. Then his shirt was undone, untucked, and her hands were on his chest, but it wasn't enough, not nearly enough. She wanted all of him, and wanted him now. "In…inside?"

"Yeah." The word tore from his throat. Cole gave Emily one last heated look of longing, then he drew away, sprinting out of the car and opening her door just as she got her shirt pulled down. They hurried into the inn like two teenagers out past curfew and rushed up the stairs to Emily's room.

As soon as they were inside, Cole spun her around and pressed her against the wall, shutting the door with his foot. His hands slid under her shirt, tugging it over her head and tossing it to the side. "God, Emily, you are beautiful."

She smiled. "Thank you."

He cupped her face with his hands and met her gaze. "I've never stopped wanting you."

The temptation to lose herself in this moment, in Cole's eyes and his touch, washed over her. She wanted him, wanted the magic they'd once had.

Even if it wasn't real.

That realization iced her desire. If she took tonight one step further with Cole, she'd be creating a fictional moment of closeness. That wasn't fair or right for either of them. If they made love, it had to be for all the right reasons—and with all the cards on the table.

This wasn't some one-night stand or a senseless fling with a stranger she'd never see again. No, this was her husband, and she was carrying his baby.

Emily drew in a fortifying breath and put her hands on Cole's chest. "Before we do anything, I have something to tell you."

He covered her hands with his. "If it's how good that burger was, I think it can wait." He started to kiss her again, but she pulled away.

"No, Cole. Please. This is something much more important."

He shifted back. "What do you need to tell me, Em?"

Now that the moment had arrived, Emily hesitated. She knew, for better or worse, that the next two words would change everything between them. Forever.

"I'm pregnant."

It took a solid minute for the words to sink into Cole's brain. They echoed in the quiet space, in his head, and his mind spiraled back through time, to another night, a hot summer evening when he'd gone over to the house on the hill and begged Emily for a second chance. They'd split a bottle of wine, and before he knew it, they were back in the bedroom and she was back in his arms, and he wasn't thinking about pregnancy or anything else but Emily.

"I thought you were on the pill," he said, and even as the words came out of his mouth, he had a feeling that was the wrong first response to such a monumental statement. But he didn't know what else to say or how to react to this.

A child. That was the one thing Cole had never wanted. A chance he'd never wanted to take. He'd told Emily someday they'd have kids because he kept thinking the further he got in life, the better chance there was that he would change his mind, but he hadn't. A little late to realize it, though.

"I was on the pill. But then we broke up and…" She shrugged. "I didn't see the point in taking it if I wasn't having sex."

"Except for that night."

She nodded. "I didn't think one night could…well, I mean, I knew it could, but I wasn't thinking about that then."

"Neither of us were."

He took a step back and ran a hand through his hair. "Pregnant?" Maybe if he repeated the word it would become real, something he could get his head around.

She nodded. "Three months along."

He kept waiting for that rush of joy, of expectation, to come over him, but it was as if Cole's guts had gone cold. No emotions filled him, nothing but shock. He nodded once, then looked at Emily. "What are you going to do about it?"

The light in her eyes dimmed, replaced by a flash of hurt, followed by the flames of anger. "What am I going to *do about it?* Trust me, Cole, you don't need to worry about that. I didn't tell you about the baby because I wanted your money or your support or anything at all from you. I'm having this baby—" as she spoke, her hand covered her belly with a protective touch "—by myself. And I am just fine with that."

"Emily, this is our child—"

"A child you never wanted. We had this conversation just the other day, and you said you didn't want to have kids, not now. Maybe not ever. I *do* want kids. I've wanted kids for a long time, and I'm okay with doing this on my own."

"We're separated. We still might end up divorced. And you think it's wise to bring a child into that?" What was she thinking? How could she do this?

Then his gaze dropped to her belly, and he realized he'd been just as much of a part of the decision. He should have stopped, should have thought. But when it came to Emily, sometimes his reason deserted him.

Now Emily was *pregnant*. The entire thing still seemed surreal, impossible.

"I didn't plan it that way, Cole. It just happened. Babies grow up in single-parent homes all the time and do just fine." She crossed to the door and pulled it open. "Look, I don't want to argue. Why don't we just get some sleep and talk about this tomorrow."

"Is this why you left? So I wouldn't find out?"

She exhaled. "I don't know. I just wanted to go somewhere else. Somewhere to think. The inn seemed like the best place to do that."

"And when were you planning on coming back?"

She knew the answer, because it had always been there, in the back of her head. She'd never admitted it out loud or to herself. Yes, she had run away, to keep from having this very conversation with Cole. To avoid the hurt. "Not until after the baby was born."

"And after you divorced me?"

She nodded. She'd thought it would be so much easier, cleaner, to end her marriage and begin this new life hundreds of mile from Cole. A cowardly move. "I was afraid, Cole, that you would try to talk me out of the divorce."

"Like I have been for the past few days."

"I just didn't want to be standing here, like we are right now, saying the things we're saying." She shook her head. Her eyes burned. Her heart ached.

"Am I that horrible of a man that you would feel like you have to leave the state to divorce me and have my child?" His voice broke, sharpened by hurt.

"No, Cole, you're not horrible at all." She clutched the door. "And that's the problem. I knew if I stayed around you, I'd fall for you all over again. And I can't do that. Not again."

"Then I'll make this easy for you, Emily." He held her gaze for a long, bittersweet moment, then Cole turned on his heel and left the room. A few minutes later, she heard the door of his room shut, followed by the sound of the front door closing, and then his rental car starting, leaving.

Cole was gone.

And even though it was what Emily had wanted and knew would happen, the sound of him leaving sent a sharp blade through her heart, severing the last strand of hope.

CHAPTER TWELVE

THE MORNING DAWNED, bright and cheery. Emily rolled over and stretched in bed, lazy, warm. Then her head cleared, the sleepiness disappeared, and she realized two things.

It was the day before Thanksgiving. And Cole had left.

What had she expected? Some big teary, emotional moment when she told him about the baby? A Hollywood moment of clarity, where he realized he wanted the baby and her, and they all went off into the sunset, happily ever after?

Nothing had changed. Cole didn't want children, and just because she was having a baby didn't mean he'd changed his mind.

She wanted to pull the covers up, stay in bed and wallow in the hurt and regret, but that would only make it worse. After a while, she rolled out of bed, pulled on a robe, bypassing her laptop and heading downstairs. On the landing, Emily paused and peered out the window at the inn's driveway, half hoping to see Cole's rental car.

But it was gone, just like it had been last night. So was Joe's car. Martin's van was in the drive, and she could hear the sound of pipes clanging in one of the bathrooms. Emily swallowed her disappointment. She'd known this was coming, asked for it to be over and told herself she was ready for the finality of her marriage, but that didn't make it any easier to take or accept.

"Good morning," Carol said when Emily entered the kitchen. Harper got to her feet and wagged her tail. "How are you feeling?"

"Terrible. But not nauseous." Emily let out a little laugh. "I finally have a morning without morning sickness, and it's a day when all I want to do is go back to bed and cry."

"Oh, Emily, I'm sorry. Do you want to talk about it?"

"Yes. No." She spied the overnighted envelope on the table, delivered that morning. "Yes."

Then she dropped into a chair at the kitchen table and poured out her heart to Carol, just like she used to when she was a teenager, and her parents were fighting and all Emily wanted was someone to listen to her and tell her it would all be okay.

She started at the beginning, telling Carol about how her marriage to Cole had started well, then slowly eroded. How she'd still had hope. How the past few days had only increased that hope and made her think maybe Cole would change his mind and want a family like she did.

"Now I'm alone, and he's gone and…" Emily sighed. "I know I'm going to be okay, but right now, it doesn't feel that way at all."

Carol's hand covered Emily's. "It'll be fine, honey. I promise."

Down the road, yes, Emily knew she had become stronger over the past few months and would, indeed, be fine, but the getting from here to there seemed an impossibly long, painful road. "He's gone, Carol. It's what I expected, and what I told him I wanted, but…"

"You also expected him to stay."

Tears rushed to Emily's eyes, spilled onto her cheeks. "Yes."

"You know, it's okay to believe in fairy tales, Emily. You always did, and I hope you always do."

Emily scoffed. "Why? They never come true."

"Maybe not. But believing that the impossible can happen is what gives our days that little bit of magic. And magic is what makes for the best stories. Don't you remember telling me that once?"

Emily smiled. She'd been a little girl when she'd said that to Carol, explaining why she loved to read fairy tales, and how when she grew up, she was going to write her own. "Are you telling me to add a happy ending to my book?"

"And to your life." Carol's fingers squeezed Emily's. "There's still magic left to be found."

The thought warmed Emily. Could there still be magic, for her? For Cole? She wasn't sure if there was any left between them, but for the first time since she'd heard his car leave the drive, she believed there'd be a happy ending for all of them. Somehow.

Her stomach rumbled, prompting Emily to head for the fridge. She reached for the orange juice, then noticed the empty middle shelf. "Carol, you don't have a turkey." She turned back. "Aren't we having Thanksgiving here?"

"To be honest, I've gotten into the habit of not making future plans." Carol sighed. "I just don't know what to do with this place. All these repairs are great, and I truly appreciate them, but..."

"You don't know whether to hold on or let go." Emily's features softened. "I can relate to that."

Carol rose and drew Emily into a hug. The embrace wrapped Emily with the same warmth and acceptance she always found at this inn, and with this woman, who was so much like a mother figure to her. "Then let's hold on together," Carol said. "At least for Thanksgiving. Because we have an awful lot to be grateful for."

Emily thought of the miracle growing inside her. "We do indeed."

Carol ran a hand through her hair, then looked around the kitchen. "Well, if we're going to have a proper Thanksgiving around here, I need to get cracking. There's a million things to do. I need to bring down the holiday dishes and—"

Emily put a hand on Carol's. "Why don't you give me a list and let me go to the store for you?"

"Are you sure?"

Emily nodded. "It'll be nice to get out for a while." And away from the reminders of Cole.

"I sure appreciate it." Carol drew a piece of paper out of the desk drawer, then started making a list. "You buy it...I'll cook it."

Emily laughed. "Deal."

The sound of clanking pipes came from up above them, followed by a muffled thud and a curse. "Uh-oh. I don't think the plumbing is cooperating with Martin. I bet he could use a little help. Maybe you should offer to go up there and help him." Emily winked.

A shy smile spread across Carol's face. "That's a darn good idea."

Emily grabbed a quick breakfast, then got ready and headed to the store. She parked outside the small grocery that passed for a supermarket in town, then grabbed a cart and started making her way through the aisles, checking off the items on Carol's list. It kept her from thinking about Cole and her future—a future that wouldn't include him.

She paused in the books and magazine aisle and allowed herself a moment to dream, to picture her novel on that shelf. Maybe not today or tomorrow, but someday, she vowed, she'd see that happen.

Her stomach cramped. The first time, she brushed the feeling off. She'd done a lot today, what with the driving and shopping and yanking that heavy turkey out of the refrigerator case. After several days of doing nothing more strenuous than working at a computer, maybe her body was complaining.

Then a second cramp, followed fast on its heels by a third. Emily fumbled in her purse for her cell phone, and dialed Carol's number. No answer. She'd probably left her phone downstairs while she helped Martin. Emily dialed the number for the inn. No answer again.

Panic rushed through Emily. What if something was wrong with the baby? Suddenly, she wanted someone here, someone to hold her hand, keep her calm. Reassure her that it would all be okay. Someone strong and sensible and composed.

She skimmed her thumb over the contacts list and then took a deep breath and called the last person in the world who wanted to deal with her or this baby.

Cole.

Cole sat at his desk and tried like hell to listen to Doug as he talked about the upcoming product launch. Any other day, he would have been asking questions, analyzing charts of age data, engaged and invested in the process.

Not today. Not one ounce of the usual excitement rose in his chest. In fact, he only heard about every other word Doug said because Cole's mind was on Emily.

His wife. The mother of his unborn child.

A child.

The word sent a combination of anticipation and fear rocketing through him. Even now, hours after Emily had told him, he wanted to both shout the news from the rooftops and run for the hills. He was a walking, talking clichéd contradiction. Him, the man who had always been decisive and driven, derailed by a human the size of a pencil eraser.

"Cole? Did you hear me?"

Cole jerked his attention back to the reports in front of him. "I'm sorry. What did you say?"

"The mid-Atlantic division is predicting a forty percent increase in sales over last year. Customer preorders are through the roof, and media buzz is strong and positive. Your idea for the screen substitution was brilliant and bought us just enough time. The Japanese supplier should be sending their first shipment next week. I think it's going to be a smooth product rollout, all in all."

"Good. Good." Cole's mind went back to Emily. What was she doing right now? Probably cursing his name three ways to the moon.

Not that he could blame her. He'd ducked out of there, using the same old excuse about work. He cleared his throat and refocused on Doug's face. "How about the mid-Atlantic? What's the report from there?"

Doug chuckled. "You must be dreaming about turkey and pie or something. Did you hear a word I just said?"

"I heard turkey and pie." Pie made him think of Emily again. Of that first awful pie she'd made him when they were newlyweds, of the late-night apple pie they'd shared and the potpie they'd made. "Uh, why would I be thinking of turkey?"

"Because Thanksgiving is tomorrow." Doug shook his head, then got to his feet. "Why don't I just email you the report? We can talk after the holiday."

"Sorry. Just having trouble getting my mind back on work after being on vacation."

"Totally understandable." Doug grinned. "Must have been a hell of a vacation to get you distracted. Wherever that place is, I want to go."

"The Gingerbread Inn," Cole said softly. "It's like one of those places you read about in a book."

Doug lingered by the door. "You going back?"

The question hit Cole hard. Was he going back? Or staying here? Returning to that empty condo with its single plate and single fork and single glass? Or going back to the big house on the hill, which brimmed with priceless artwork and antiques, yet still felt as empty as a tomb? Or going back to the run-down inn by the lake, where the sunshine warmed his back and good home cooking filled his belly? Where he'd had his best sleep in years. And where the woman he had always loved slept with their baby growing inside her.

"I don't know," Cole said. "I'm not sure there's still a vacancy for me."

Doug laughed. "You're Cole Watson. You built this company from your kitchen table to this." He gave an expansive wave. "When has something that simple stood in your way?"

After Doug was gone, Cole sat in his office and looked around the room. He'd done what Doug had said, built his company from an idea he'd had in that cramped New York apartment, to this. A global leader, an innovator, all those buzzwords people threw out.

He'd worked so hard, spent so many hours here, because he thought those words mattered. Thought all of *this*—the walls, the employees, the profits—mattered. He'd kept reaching for a goal he couldn't see, a goal that moved every time he approached it, because he thought it would fill that driving need deep inside him to succeed. To have it all.

He had the luxury cars. The custom-made mansion on a hill. The fat bank account. What he didn't have was a wife and a marriage.

Everything here was stuff. Inanimate objects. He'd dedicated his life to—

Nothing that mattered, not in the long run.

Damn. How could such a smart man get it so abysmally wrong?

There was a double tap on his door, and Irene poked her head in his office. "Cole? Emily called. She's been trying to reach you."

He yanked his cell out of the holster. "Damn. I had the sound off while I was in the meeting. Let me call her back."

"No, you need to leave." She bustled into the room, grabbed his overcoat off the coat tree and pressed it into his hands. "I already called a car service to take you to the airport. Emily is in the hospital."

"In the hospital?" Cole's heart stopped. He stared at Irene, absorbing the words. His heart didn't beat. His lungs didn't breathe. His brain didn't function. He heard the words again and—

Then he ran.

* * *

Emily shivered in the room, even though the stark white hospital room was kept at a warmer than normal temp. She drew the covers up to her chest and flicked off the television. Only a few channels, and not much to watch on any of them. Her hand went to her abdomen, and she sent up a silent prayer, then closed her eyes and lay back against the firm pillow.

The door opened, but she kept her eyes shut, sure it was the nurse back again to check on her roommate, an older woman given to pushing the nurse button every five minutes. But when she didn't hear any sound from the space next to her, Emily opened her eyes and found Cole standing there, his face ashen, sweat beading on his brow. "Are you okay?" she asked.

"Are you okay?" he said at the same time.

Her heart leaped at the sight of him and the concern on his face. "I'm fine, or I will be. I'm sorry for calling you. I couldn't get ahold of Carol and I didn't have Joe's number and I was scared and…" She shook her head. Calling him had been a mistake. She never should have told Irene she was in the hospital. "It was ridiculous to think you could do anything from all the way in New York. I ended up having the store manager drive me—"

"Is everything okay?"

She nodded. "Just a little preterm labor. The baby's jumping the gun. It's nothing to worry about. Happens all the time. I just have to take it easy for a little while."

Cole exhaled. "Good. I'm glad you're okay."

She noticed he didn't mention the baby. God, why was she such a fool? Calling him, thinking an emergency would change anything? "You can go back to New York. I'm sorry."

He was by her bedside in three fast strides. "Number one, never apologize for calling me when you need me. Regardless of how things go between us, I want you to know that you can always rely on me."

The words *regardless of how things go between us* filled Emily with a bone-deep sadness. For all her talk about divorce, she'd realized in the past few days that a part of her didn't want a divorce at all. She wanted to work things out with Cole, for the two of them to celebrate their baby's arrival and find a new marriage, one where they were there for each other, rather than running along parallel but diverging tracks.

She wanted her husband, damn it.

"Number two," he went on, "if you are sick or in the hospital or anything like that, I want to know about it. I will always watch out for you and care for you, Emily. No matter what."

"Okay. I'll remember that." She shifted against the pillows and sat up. The sheet slipped down, exposing the ugly hospital gown underneath. She was sure her hair was a mess, her makeup smeared and for the first time in a long time, Emily wished she had looked in a mirror before Cole came.

Like a nice hairstyle and neat eyeliner would change anything. She needed to face reality. He hadn't changed his mind and she hadn't changed hers.

"Thanks," she said. "Anyway—"

"I'm not finished." Cole took another step forward.

He stood alongside the bed now, his hip within touching distance of her hand. A part of her wished he would sit on the edge of the bed and just talk to her. Like he had in the past few days.

Then she remembered his reaction to the pregnancy and told herself to stop wishing for things that would never be.

"Number three," Cole said, "I'm staying

with you until this baby is born. If there are complications—"

"Nothing I can't handle, Cole. I don't need your help. I can stay with Carol until the baby comes. She could use the extra set of hands, I'm sure." Emily didn't add that she'd been put on modified bed rest for the next several weeks, to stop the early labor contractions. The doctor had told her to reduce stress, not to lift anything heavy and to rest. So far, she wasn't doing well at two out of three of those.

"At least let me hire a nurse to—"

"No. I'll be fine." She didn't want his money or his pity, or anything other than him. Unfortunately, that was the one thing he wasn't offering.

He let out a breath. "Why won't you let me take care of you?"

She leaned forward in the bed and faced Cole. "Because it's not your job anymore." Then she leaned over, tugged out the envelope in her purse and showed him the papers she had had overnighted to her this morning. If she couldn't stick to her resolve to be done with Cole when she was around him, then she had to do something concrete about ending her marriage. "I called my lawyer and he got the papers together for me to file for divorce."

Cole's blue eyes filled with hurt, then the hurt gave way to an icy coldness. "Is that what you really want?"

"Yes." God, she wished he would just leave the room. She wanted to cry, to be alone, to face the fact that her husband didn't want the baby—or the life—that she so desperately did.

"What if something happens to you or…" He waved at her stomach.

That gesture and his avoidance of the word *baby* told her everything she needed to know. "*We* are no longer your concern. Goodbye, Cole." Then she turned over and curled into a ball. She held her tears until she heard the soft click of the door.

Cole didn't answer his phone. He didn't talk to Joe or Carol. He didn't go back to New York.

He had the driver bring him to the inn, then he headed straight out to the gazebo in the back. Cole ripped off his suit jacket, tossing it on the ground, heedless of the price tag of the custom-made suit. Then he started tearing out the old posts from the rotted outbuilding, yanking, kicking, doing whatever it took to wrench the ruined posts out of place. Joe brought down the new wood and laid it on the deck of the gazebo without a word. He returned with a toolbox, laid that beside the wood. Cole kept on working, taking his frustrations out on the decrepit gazebo. After several trips back and forth with supplies, Joe finally went back to the inn, sensing that Cole wanted to be alone.

Except that was the whole problem. He didn't *want* to be alone. He wanted to be with Emily. And she wanted nothing to do with him.

He'd sent a car and driver to the hospital to drive her back to the inn. Hired a nurse to stay with her. Emily had dismissed them both, Cole had been told, and opted to take a taxi instead. When he heard the car's tires on the gravel drive, he stopped working. But Emily walked into the inn and never even looked his way.

What the hell was he doing here? Why didn't he just give up already?

"Here. Take a break." Joe dangled a beer in front of Cole.

Cole shook his head. "I gotta get this done."

"No, you gotta take a break before you have a heart attack."

Cole wiped the sweat off his brow. He was breathing heavy and his arms ached. It wasn't the good, job-well-done ache he'd had over the past few days. No, this was the pain of a self-induced beating by carpentry. Damn, he'd screwed everything up. What was that about good intentions? His hadn't led him anywhere he wanted to go.

He let out a sigh, then put down his sledge-hammer and took a seat beside Joe on the floor of the gazebo. "What am I doing here?"

"Damned if I know." Joe took a sip of his beer. "If I were you, I'd just leave. She doesn't want you here."

Cole cursed. What did Joe know? Where did he get off saying that, anyway? "She's just confused."

"Dude, she's not confused. She knows what she wants. *You're* the one who's confused."

"I'm not goddamn leaving and I'm not god-damned confused."

"Then leave."

"I told you I'm not—"

Joe leaned in with a grin on his face that said his reverse psychology had had the de-sired effect. "If you aren't going to leave," Joe said, "then you better damned well start to fight."

Cole took a long sip of beer and thought about the past few days and the river of con-tradictory emotions running through him ever since Emily had told him about the pregnancy. "I just don't think I'm ready for kids."

"Hell, who is? They are the most inconvenient creatures in the world, but I hear they're pretty cool to have."

"Yeah, for some people." Cole put the beer aside and got to his feet. He wanted to take Joe's advice and fight for his marriage, but even if he did, where would that leave them? Together, but with a baby on the way. A child, who would look to Cole for love and guidance. For him to be not just a father, but a *good* father.

The one thing he had no idea how to do.

"I gotta get back to work. Sooner I get these projects finished, the sooner I can go back to New York."

"What's stopping you from leaving now? Just hiring this out?"

"I made a commitment to finishing. I keep those commitments." Okay, so that was a lie. He was here because he wanted to make sure Emily was okay.

"Is that why you don't want to get divorced? Because you committed to finishing the marriage?" Joe took a step forward. "Or because you don't want to lose the best woman to ever come along in your life?"

"Will you just let me finish this gazebo? And quit with the questions?" They were the same questions Cole had asked himself and didn't have any answers for then or now.

Joe shook his head. "You are being an idiot, Cole. You're a smart man, hell, a genius some would say the way you built that business up from nothing. But right now you are being the biggest idiot on the East Coast." Then he grabbed his beer and headed up the hill.

CHAPTER THIRTEEN

PROPPED UP AGAINST the pillows on her bed, Emily sat with her laptop open on her lap and the book file waiting for her input. The packet from her lawyer sat beside her on the floral comforter, also waiting. All it required was a signature, and then the divorce was in process.

Even after everything, she had yet to sign the paper. She still had hope, damn it.

Because she'd seen a little of the old Cole in the past few days. For a long time, she'd given up, thinking the man she remembered from those early days had been sucked into a demanding job and a never-ending drive toward success. But the Cole who had fixed the steps and made the pie and given her the journal was the Cole she had fallen in love with years ago.

And damn it all, the same Cole she still loved.

She went to the window and watched him

working on the gazebo like a man possessed. When he'd left the hospital earlier, she had fully expected him to go back to New York. And yet he was here.

Why?

The day had edged into late afternoon, the sun sinking lower and lower in the sky. A cold front was moving in, according to the weather reports. The nice fall days would be over, and soon winter would clamp its snowy grip over the inn. Tomorrow was Thanksgiving, one of her favorite holidays of the year, and the first one in forever that would be filled with home-made food, not a catered turkey. It was the kind of back-to-basics life that she wanted for her child.

A life a thousand miles away from the one Cole wanted.

And that, in the end, was the reality she had yet to accept.

Emily drew on a thick sweater and went downstairs. Carol was sitting by the fireplace, curled up in a chair and reading a book. "How are you feeling?" she asked.

"Much better. I think I just needed some rest."

"Well, you can get plenty of that here."

Carol put her book on the side table. "How are you doing emotionally?"

"I don't know." Emily's gaze went to the window. It was getting too dark to see all the way past the trees to the gazebo, but she suspected Cole was still out there, working. "I have a lot of decisions to make."

Carol got to her feet and grabbed an anorak jacket off the hook on the wall. "Why don't you go for a walk before dinner? A little fresh air always makes everything clearer. This is probably one of the last nice nights you'll have around here before the snow starts flying."

"Don't you need help prepping for Thanksgiving tomorrow? I should—"

"You are not supposed to be doing any such thing, missy. You worry about that precious little gift right there—" Carol gestured to Emily's abdomen "—and nothing else. Okay?"

Emily drew Carol into a tight hug. "Thank you."

"No, *thank you*," Carol said, her voice thick with emotion. "You've given me back the one thing I lost."

"What's that?"

Carol drew back and cupped Emily's face with a tender, maternal touch. This was why Emily had always been so drawn to the warm and giving innkeeper. She was more like a mother to Emily than the woman who shared Emily's DNA.

"Hope," Carol said. "I was ready to give up on this place before you came here."

"I couldn't let you do that," Emily said. "This place is home to me."

"No, honey, that's where you're wrong. This place isn't home. Home is where the people you love are. Whether they're in New York or Paris or the Gingerbread Inn." Carol drew the coat closed and pressed a kiss to Emily's forehead. "Now go for that walk."

Emily thanked Carol, then headed outside. She didn't hear any sounds of work and figured Cole had left after all. Just as well, she told herself, if only so she wouldn't give room to the disappointment churning inside her.

Emily walked down the crushed stone path that led from the inn to the lake, her way guided by little landscape lights. It looked almost magical, with the tiny lights against the stark darkness.

"It's so peaceful out here, isn't it?"

She turned at the sound of Cole's voice. Not startled. A part of her knew he hadn't left. Had hoped he had stayed. Because of her and the baby? Or just because he wanted to win the argument of hiring a nursemaid to look after her? "Yes, it is."

"Mind if I walk with you?" he asked.

"Not at all."

They started toward the dock, then detoured to walk the edge of the lake, traversing the path that the teenage lovers had probably taken all those years ago. Except this time, Emily wasn't running away with Cole like the teenagers had.

No, she was finally going to tell him it was over. She had tried, over and over, to make this work. But he had yet to open up to her, nor did he have any interest in raising their child with her. Those two things gave her the answers she needed. Answers she needed to accept once and for all.

"First, I want to apologize," he said. "I reacted badly to you telling me about the baby. You took me by surprise. I never expected—"

"That we'd make love and I could get pregnant?"

"Yeah. Guess I need to repeat high school health class." He walked a while longer, a tall man silhouetted in the dark. "How did we get to this point, Emily? How did we let it go so wrong for so long, and never do anything about it?"

"I don't know, Cole. I really don't." She looked out at the lake, twinkling under the light cast by the crescent moon. She thought of all those dreams she'd had years before, and how far away she'd got from those wishes. "When I was younger, the other girls and I stood here at the edge of the lake and made a promise to each other because of these rocks we'd found. Remember the one I showed you?"

He nodded.

"We thought those rocks were a sign. Of what, I'm not sure, but we decided that day to promise that we would always follow our dreams. I made the promise, and then I didn't keep it. Yeah, I wrote some in high school and college, but once we got married and you started making enough money that I didn't have to work, I didn't go back to writing. I kept finding other things to do, excuses, really, for why I couldn't write. It wasn't just about being afraid of rejection, it was about—" she let out a breath "—failing. If I didn't try, then I couldn't fail, you know what I mean?"

He let out a short, dry laugh. "More than you know."

"Then Melissa died, and we all got these letters from her. I realized that my life was ticking by and I was desperately unhappy, but I hadn't done anything about it. I just kept waiting for things to change, instead of taking the leap and making the change myself."

She had done the same thing with her marriage. Letting it fall apart rather than confronting the issues—and possibly failing. Her inaction had fed into her greatest fear, and now the dreams she'd had when she walked down the aisle with Cole had died.

"And those changes are what brought you here," Cole said.

She nodded. "I thought it was appropriate to go back to the place where the dream began. Plus the inn has served as a nice, quiet retreat, a good place to write my book, to think and to get away."

"From me." The two words were exhaled on a curt note.

"That was the plan." She gave him a crooked smile. "I never imagined you'd follow me."

"I never imagined you'd leave." He took her hand in his. "I guess I thought that this whole separation would blow over, and things would go back to the way they were. I never realized how unhappy you were."

"I should have spoken up more." She'd let fear rule her choices for too long. If there was one thing she'd learned in the months on her own, it was that she was stronger and able to weather more storms than she thought.

"I should have paid better attention to you and to us," Cole said. "I kept my focus on the wrong things. On the company, instead of on our relationship. I looked around my office this morning and realized all of that was stuff. Things that I had worked to achieve. At the cost of our marriage." He sighed. "That was too high of a price to pay for a better bottom line."

Hearing him say that filled her with a thrill. Her heart had never given up on Cole. Still, her brain raised a caution flag. They had a baby on the way, and that introduced a whole other dynamic. Cole had yet to talk about the baby. It was as if he thought ignoring her pregnancy would keep them from having to deal with it. In a few months, Sweet Pea would be here and there'd be no ignoring him or her then. "I guess we were both looking in the wrong direction. Now I'm just looking ahead, to the baby coming."

He started walking some more, his shoes making impressions in the not-yet-frozen earth. "You asked me why I didn't want kids. I kept telling you, and myself, that it was all about it being the right time, but that's not it."

She waited, afraid to press, afraid of what she might hear next. When he didn't continue, she said, "Then what was it, Cole?"

"I don't talk about my past, Em." He ran a hand through his hair. "With anyone."

"You told Joe."

"Kinda hard not to. We've been friends forever, and he was at my house a few times when I was younger. He saw what went on." Cole cursed and shook his head. "Let's just say it wasn't pretty."

She swung around in front of him and took his hands. "Tell me, Cole. I'm your wife. I should be your best friend, too. That means knowing the good and the bad about you."

"Do you know why I never told you about my childhood?"

She shook her head.

"Because I'm *ashamed* of it, Emily." His voice sharpened, rose. "I never wanted you to be anything but proud of me. I'm supposed to be the man, the one who leads the family, takes on the challenges—"

She cut off his words with a soft hand against his cheek. "You don't always have to be the strong one, Cole."

His features crumpled, and he turned away. She let him go, sensing that the conversation had brought up something Cole had kept tucked away for a long, long time. A loon called out from the other side of the lake, and a fish flopped its tail against the water. Then Cole turned back, and when he spoke again, his voice had gone hoarse. "I don't know any other way to be, Em."

Her heart broke for her strong, smart, driven husband, who kept all those vulnerable parts of himself behind a tough shell. A facade. "Just be yourself, Cole. That's all I ever wanted."

"I don't even know if I know how to do that. I have no map, no guidebook. I know how to be the best at school or work, but I haven't a clue how to be the best parent."

"Most people don't, Cole. You figure it out as you go along."

"What if I figure it out wrong?" He ran a hand through his hair, then gestured toward a large rock at the edge of the water. They sat down together, facing the lake. Cole took Emily's hand in both of his and rubbed her fingers, providing warmth, protection from the cold.

"Tell me," she repeated, softer this time. "Please."

Maybe then she'd understand him. Maybe

then she'd know enough to move forward, in one direction or the other.

Cole paused for so long, his gaze on the soft ripples in the water, that she was afraid he wasn't going to say anything at all. He picked up a handful of rocks and flung one at the lake. It skipped twice, then sank beneath the surface. "My mom started drinking when I was a little boy. She was in a car accident, and I think she drank because of the pain from that. Maybe she drank because it sucked to live with my father. I'm not sure. We never talked about it. But she stopped being any kind of mother to me long before I was in kindergarten."

"Oh, Cole, that's awful."

He shrugged, as if it hadn't bothered him, but she could see the pain in his eyes, in the hunch of his shoulders. To live without a mother at such a young age, no one to kiss his scrapes or tell him bedtime stories, had to have been incredibly tough. Her tough husband, made that way by a childhood as rough as cement.

"My father was a...difficult man," Cole went on. "After my mother started drinking, he got worse. Maybe it was because his world was out of control, so he tried to control it more, through me. I'm not sure. But he had incredibly high standards for me to meet, and there was no choice but to meet them. An A wasn't good enough, it had to be an A+. My room had to pass a military-type inspection. Hell, before I went to school, he would bring me in the kitchen and inspect my clothes, my nails, my hair. If anything was out of place, I'd be punished. I learned not to make mistakes. Ever."

Cole flinched, as if dodging an invisible blow. Emily wasn't sure if he even knew he'd done it. Her heart broke, and she wished she could go back in time and protect the little boy Cole had once been. Stop the bully who had the name Dad and tell Cole it was okay to get dirty, to make messes, to have fun. Take away the bruises and the tears and hug him tight. "Oh, Cole."

"My mother never spoke up or stopped him or did anything but drink more and more and more. So I decided the only way to keep my father happy was to be the best. Never to quit. And always, always to win." He nearly spat the words.

It explained so much about Cole, about his approach to work, to life. To them. "And never to admit a weakness," she added softly.

"Exactly."

"Cole." She shifted on the rock and reached up to trace the features she loved so much, to meet his gaze with her own. Even now, he held himself stoic and strong, as if relating someone else's story. It was a defense, she realized, against more blows. The physical hits may have stopped, but the emotional ones still came at him. "It's not a weakness to need someone."

He jerked away and got to his feet as if the very concept burned him. "It is to me, Emily. I never told you about any of this because I was ashamed of my parents. Of the way I grew up. I didn't want you to pity me or—"

"See you as weak?"

He nodded.

"That's where you're wrong. To me, you are the strongest man in the world because you didn't just survive that past, you *conquered* it."

"I didn't conquer it, Emily. That's the problem. I'm still scared as hell that I'll become my father with my own children." He shook his head and cursed under his breath. The loon called a second time, as if searching for a friend in the cold, dark night. Cole got to his feet and dumped the rest of the rocks onto the ground. "I can't do that to our baby, Emily.

Maybe we should do the right thing and just go our separate ways. I'll take care of you financially—"

"Stop, Cole." She wanted to hug him and hit him all at the same time. How could he be so smart and yet so incredibly dumb? "Do you know what the problem is? You're just as afraid of failure as I am."

"I'm not afraid. I'm trying to be sensible."

She let out a gust. "Let me know when you want to stop being sensible and lead with your heart instead of your brain. Do you think I'm not terrified that I'll be a terrible mother? But I love this baby enough already—" her hand went to her abdomen "—to take that chance and to do my best. I'm okay with not being perfect all the time. Life and love are messy, Cole. Like the ties on the closet floor. When you're ready to stop being afraid of a mess, you know where me and your baby will be."

Then she drew her coat closed and headed back into the inn. The light fog had drifted in from the lake, and now swirled around her feet and legs as she walked, as if begging her to give love a second chance.

CHAPTER FOURTEEN

THE PHONE ON the other end rang a half dozen times before it was answered with a flurry of laughter, voices and a barking dog. "Hello?"

"Hey, Pete, it's your big brother." Cole perched on the windowsill of his hotel room in Boston. He should have gone back to New York, but until he was sure Emily was going to be okay, he couldn't bring himself to leave the state. Several stories below, the traffic passed by in a steady stream. People headed out of town to visit friends and family, to share hugs and pie. A holiday he had avoided, finding excuse after excuse to work or be out of town, because he hadn't understood the importance of being grateful for those he loved. Until now. Until he'd lost them.

Now he had a family on the way. And where was he? In a hotel instead of sitting around a Thanksgiving table with Emily.

"Cole!" Pete's voice boomed over the phone. "Long time no hear."

"Too long." Yet another personal relationship that had suffered because of Cole's constant devotion to the company. He vowed to change that from here on out. "Sorry about that. I wanted to call, wish you a happy Thanksgiving."

"Same to you. One of these years, I'll get you to come down to Connecticut for the craziness of our house." Pete shushed the barking dog. "Sorry. Got the wife's entire family here, and our Lab thinks they're all here to visit him. The kids are all excited, probably because they know if we're eating turkey it means Christmas is just around the corner." Pete laughed, an easygoing sound.

Everything about Cole's younger brother was easier and simpler than Cole. The younger Watson had an affable personality, one that rarely stressed about anything. Maybe because Cole had done enough worrying for the both of them when they'd been younger. Cole had done his best to take the brunt of their father's temper, to spare Pete. "How is Diane? The kids?"

"Everyone's great. Our youngest turns two next week, and the oldest is a star in first grade. I think she inherited your genius tendencies."

Cole chuckled. "I am far from a genius."

"Yeah, well, I disagree. You were always smarter than me." Pete's voice softened with love and affection. "So how's Emily?"

Cole didn't want to get into the messy details with his brother. He hadn't called for that, or to talk about how worried Cole was that he was too late to repair the damage in his marriage. "She's great. And, uh, she's expecting."

"A baby? That's fabulous, Cole, really fabulous. I'm thrilled for you. You must be over the moon."

Cole shifted on the sill and put his back to the window. "Can I ask you something?"

"Sure. Anything."

Cole fiddled with the phone cord. "Were you ever afraid you'd turn out like Dad or Mom when you had your first child?"

The busy noise in the background faded away. There was a soft click, which meant Pete had probably ducked into another room to talk in private. "Hell, yes. Of course I was. With parents like ours, you'd have to be a fool not to worry at least some of that would rub off."

"How did you move past it? Finally take the plunge and have kids?"

Pete chuckled. "It's ironic, you know, you asking me for advice. I've always looked up to you, big brother, to be the leader, the one to tell me what to do."

"I know how to ace a test, launch a business, grow a market share, but when it comes to having a family..." Cole exhaled. "I don't know where to start."

"You start with *love,* Cole," Pete said quietly. "If you love your kids, everything else flows from there."

"Mom and Dad loved us, in their own way, I'm sure. How is that any different?"

"They put other things ahead of that love. Alcohol. Success. Appearances. They led with the least important thing rather than the most important."

Cole thought about that for a minute. It was a concept that applied to business, too. Focus on the most critical areas first, then the other, less-important things would fall into place. "That makes perfect sense."

"Even as the goofball of the family, I can come out with a smart line or two." Pete chuckled. "Hey, the natives are pounding on the door. Turkey's ready and waiting for me to show off my carving skills, and if I don't get in there soon, they're going to riot." Then Pete's voice softened, the little brother worried about the older brother. "You going somewhere for Thanksgiving?"

Cole looked out the window again, but his gaze went farther than the roads he could see. To a cozy, quaint inn deep in Massachusetts. "I'm going home, Pete. Home."

Emily was awake before dawn, the urge to write burning inside her. Her fingers flew across the keyboard, fast and furious, the page count adding up at a rapid pace. A little after eleven, she sat back and let out a sigh. The book needed a lot of revisions yet, but the gist of the story was down. She had written more in these past few days than she had in her entire life. And it felt good, really good.

For an hour, she read, and as she turned the pages in the manuscript, she realized she had told her life story in her characters. The woman struggling to find her place in a marriage that had gone dead, the husband who couldn't give up on the way things used to be. But unlike her own life, her characters had found their way out of the quicksand and back to each other. If only her real life could read as smoothly as the novel did.

The scent of roasted turkey and fresh-baked

pies drew Emily's attention, and she put the novel aside. Emily showered, dressed, then headed downstairs. It was Thanksgiving Day. Instead of spending it at the house in New York, eating a catered dinner by herself or with friends while Cole worked and ate at his desk, she was here, at the inn, with Carol, Martin and Joe, her makeshift family.

The only person missing was Cole. Emily told herself that he was the one missing out, the one who would be alone. Still, her heart ached. She paused on the landing, looking for Cole's car. But it wasn't there.

She pressed a hand to her belly. "We'll be okay, Sweet Pea. I promise."

She found Martin and Joe in the living room, watching a football game and talking about things like field goals and Hail Mary passes. Emily ducked into the kitchen and sneaked a fresh-baked biscuit just as Carol turned around. "Hey, no snacking," Carol said.

Emily grinned. "How can I resist fresh-baked bread? Besides, this wasn't for me. It was for the baby."

Carol laughed. "In that case, take a second one."

"Oh, I will. And I'll also have an extra helping of pie. Or two." Emily picked up a whisk and began stirring the gravy. "It all looks awesome, Carol. You are an incredible cook."

"If you want, I can teach you. If you're planning on staying."

Where else was Emily going to go? The house in New York had never been home. This inn came the closest to the warm and loving environment Emily wanted for Sweet Pea. It also offered the perfect refuge for a woman trying to get over a painful divorce. "I'll be here as long as you'll have me," Emily said.

Carol drew her into a one-armed hug. "You're welcome to stay as long as you want."

"Thanks, Carol." The two of them worked together for the next few minutes. Well, Carol worked, and made Emily sit down and do nothing more strenuous than stirring the gravy. Emily tried not to think about Cole's absence, or wonder about whether he was at the office or the big house in New York. All she knew was that he wasn't here. With her.

She cooked and laughed and chatted, but deep inside, disappointment sat like a chunk of concrete. This was what it would be like when the divorce was final. A part of her aware of the empty space at her side, while she forced a smile to her face and feigned happiness. Someday, it would get easier. Someday.

An hour later, they took seats around the dining room table, with the turkey in the center as the star of the meal. Carol sat at the head, Martin to her right and Joe beside him, while Emily sat across from the men and kept her gaze averted from the empty chair beside her.

"Let's all join hands and say thanks," Carol said. The four of them did as she asked, holding hands across their table and bowing their heads. "Thank you, God, for bringing us all together," Carol said, "and thank you for good food and good friends. I am grateful on this day of thanks for the support and help of friends. People like Martin, Joe and Emily."

"I'm grateful for an invitation to a great meal with a beautiful woman," Martin said.

Carol giggled. "Thank you, Martin."

"I'm grateful to be eating a home-cooked meal with some of the best people I know," Joe said. "There's nowhere else I'd want to be today."

Emily opened her mouth to speak, but before she could say anything, she heard a noise behind her.

"I'm grateful for second chances," said a deep baritone voice. "I'm also unbelievably grateful for my wife and for the child she's carrying."

Cole's voice, coming from right beside her. For a second, Emily thought maybe she had wished so hard for him to be here that she had imagined the sound and the words she had wanted to hear. She opened her eyes and looked to her left. Cole stood there, in a pale blue button-down shirt and a pair of jeans, looking relaxed and sexy. He gave her a smile, and her heart flipped over.

Cole.

That man loves you more than anything in the world.

Emily drew her hand out of Joe's, waited for Cole to slide into the seat, then take her hand in his, warm, secure, like coming home. His finger drifted over the ring she'd put back on her finger this morning. He looked up with surprise in his eyes, then gave her a tender, sweet smile. Her heart caught and her throat closed. "I'm grateful for miracles," she said.

"And I'm grateful as hell that it's time to eat now that we're all here. Finally," Joe said with a nod in Cole's direction. Everyone laughed, and they broke apart, sending around the dishes family style while Carol carved the turkey and loaded everyone up with moist, tender slices topped with smooth, steaming gravy. The five of them chatted and laughed during the meal. As Emily looked around at the faces of those who were dear to her, she thought it had to be the best Thanksgiving she'd ever had.

When they were done, Carol shooed Emily and Cole out of the house, insisting the other two could do the cleanup. Emily and Cole grabbed their coats, then ducked out into the chilly evening air. They walked down the same lighted path she had taken the night before, though it felt like a million years ago. Had something changed? Had Cole changed his mind? Did she dare to hope just one more time?

As they neared the lake, Emily bit back a laugh. No wonder Carol had urged the two of them to go outside. Carol still believed in happily ever after—and in the power of old legends.

A soft gauzy fog came off the lake, a combination of the still-warm water and the cold bite in the air. It drifted over the water like a ghostly blanket, reaching long delicate tendrils across the grassy banks.

"It looks amazing, doesn't it?" Cole said.

"Almost magical. As if anything can happen tonight."

"Like a dream," she said. She drew her coat tighter around her. Winter was nipping at their heels, if the bite in the air was any indication.

Cole came around in front of her, opened his own coat and drew her into the warmth of his chest. She was so tempted to stay here, warm and protected, forever. Instead, she stepped back.

"I...I can't, Cole," she said. The words scraped her throat, ached in her heart. "I can't keep getting close then breaking apart. It hurts too much. I mean, I'm glad you came today, but you're just going to leave, and I can't do this anymore." She strode down the dock before the tears in her eyes made it to the surface and undid all her resolve. "I know what you said, but my God, it is so hard for me to trust you. To trust us."

Cole caught up to her and captured her hand. "Don't go, Emily. Please."

She spun toward him. The fog licked at the edges of the dock, as if they were standing in a cauldron. "I can't do this," she said again. "I just can't."

"And I can't live without you. Or our baby."

Those last words stopped her. She swallowed hard, sure she had heard him wrong. That was twice today that he had mentioned the baby. Did that mean he had changed his mind about wanting a family? "You…what?"

Instead of answering, he lifted her left hand to the light. The tiny diamond Cole had given her years ago sparkled in the moonlight. He'd tried to buy her a bigger ring when he made his first million, but she had always preferred the simple small stone. "Why did you put your ring back on?"

She gave a little shrug and a wry smile crossed her face. "No matter how hard I tried, I couldn't give up on us. Or on you. I keep trying, Lord knows I do, but I guess I started believing in happy endings a long time ago, and I just can't stop." Tears brimmed in her eyes, and her fingers closed around his. "You're a good man, Cole Watson, and I always thought I was lucky to marry you."

"Ah, Em, how is it that you always see the best in me?" He brushed away a tendril of hair from her face, his touch so tender, so light.

"Because I'm your wife," she said, "and because…I love you."

His eyes lit, and a smile curved across his face. "Do you? Still?"

"I never stopped." It was the truth and one

of the many things she had been afraid to say. Where had that fear got her? Nowhere but filled with regret. If Cole walked away at the end of this, so be it. She would know she had given their marriage every last possible chance. "I've always loved you, Cole. I always will. You stole my heart the day we met, and I've never asked for it back."

"I love you, too, Emily. I love the way you smile, the way your eyes light up when you're excited, the way you curve into me when you're cold. I love your cooking and your messes and your laugh. I just didn't realize how much I loved you, or how deep that love ran inside my heart…until I thought I lost you." His hand reached up again, and his blue eyes locked on hers. "I haven't, have I? Lost you?"

She shook her head, her vision blurring behind the tears. No matter how many times she had said she was done, her heart had never got the message. She still loved her husband, still wanted him. Still wanted to wake up next to him and build a life with their child. "No, Cole. I'm still here."

"Good." He exhaled a long breath of relief. "That's so damned good to hear. The whole way over here, I was so sure I was too late.

That you had already signed the papers and moved on in your heart."

She wanted to linger in this moment of connection, in the joy in Cole's eyes, but she couldn't, not until she brought up the one topic they had thus far avoided tonight. "I haven't signed the papers. And I won't, until I'm sure."

"Sure about what?"

She watched the fog undulate across the lake, slow and soft, like a gossamer blanket. On a night many years in the past, two young lovers had stood at the edge of this very lake and taken a giant risk to find their own happy ending.

"I'm still having our baby, and if you don't want to be a real family, I can't stay with you." Emily placed a hand on her abdomen. "Sweet Pea and me are a package deal."

"Sweet Pea?"

She shrugged. "It's what I named the baby until I know whether it's a boy or a girl."

"I like that name. A lot." He took a step forward, his face filled with tentative curiosity. He put out a hand. "Can I?"

She moved her hand away and gave him a nod. "You can't feel anything yet."

Cole's palm was warm, even through her jeans, though when his palm met the tiny bulge of her belly, it seemed as if she and Cole were joined in a deeper way than they ever had been before. Cole lifted his gaze to hers. "When will it start kicking?"

"A couple more months. By then, I'll be fat and ugly."

"You will never ever be ugly, Emily. You are the most beautiful woman in the world."

"And you are the most biased man on the planet."

He chuckled. "Maybe so."

She covered his hand with hers, then drew in a deep breath. "Tell me, Cole, do you want to take the biggest risk of your life and become a father?"

He lifted his gaze to hers, and for the first time ever, she saw trepidation in Cole's eyes. "What if I'm like my own father?"

"You won't be."

"How do you know that?"

She thought a moment, looking for the right words to show him what she saw when she looked at him through her eyes. "Because you ate that terrible chicken and potatoes dinner I made with a smile on your face. Because you made love with me in the messy closet. And most of all, because you are a man who would never hurt anyone you love."

"Ah, but I have hurt you, Emily. Too many times to count." He cupped her jaw and studied her face. "I never meant to. I thought I was building a life for us. I never realized all that time at work was destroying our life at the same time."

She thought of the envelope in her room. The papers that needed only a signature to take that final step to dissolving her marriage. "Where do we go from here, Cole? How do I know that if we get back together, you won't go back to working a thousand hours a week? I want a family, Cole. That means dinners at home and road trips in the summer and picnics in the park."

He reached in his pocket and took out his phone. The screen lit with messages and alerts, as busy as ever, even on a holiday. "This is where we go, Em." He leaned back, then pitched his arm forward. The phone spiraled through the air, then disappeared in the thickening fog before landing in the lake with a heavy plop. A second later, it disappeared under the surface.

She stared at the space where the phone had been, openmouthed. "Why…why would you do that?"

"Because nothing matters more to me than

you. Us." His hand went to her belly again. "All of us."

"Really?"

"Really. I've been a fool for too damned long. And I'm not going to be that stupid for one second longer." He cupped her jaw with his hands and brought his mouth within inches. "I love you, Emily. I love our baby. I want to marry you again and do it right this time."

"But how do we fix everything? Where do we begin?"

"We begin with love. Everything else will flow from that. I promise." Then he drew his wife into his arms and kissed her while the fog wrapped around them, and once again the lake's decades-old legend brought two lovers together, this time in a happy ending.

* * * * *

#4399 PROPOSAL AT THE LAZY S RANCH
Slater Sisters of Montana
by Patricia Thayer

When a snowstorm blows in, childhood sweethearts Josie and Garrett are stranded together. Old attractions come flooding back—but this time, there's nowhere to run....

#4400 A LITTLE BIT OF HOLIDAY MAGIC
by Melissa McClone

Grace Wilcox has already loved and lost one hero. Can she really let herself get close to firefighter Bill Paulson—even if it is Christmas?

#4401 A CADENCE CREEK CHRISTMAS
Cadence Creek Cowboys
by Donna Alward

Brooding rancher Rhys is surprised to find himself falling for gorgeous Taylor Shepard. Could she be the Christmas present he never even knew he wanted?

#4402 MARRY ME UNDER THE MISTLETOE
The Gingerbread Girls
by Rebecca Winters

Single dad Rick Jenner is trying as hard as possible to forget Andrea's beautiful eyes. But when you wish upon a star, anything can happen!

HRLPCNM1013

REQUEST YOUR FREE BOOKS!

2 FREE NOVELS
FROM THE ROMANCE COLLECTION
PLUS 2 FREE GIFTS!

YES! Please send me 2 FREE novels from the Romance Collection and my 2 FREE gifts (gifts are worth about $10). After receiving them, if I don't wish to receive any more books, I can return the shipping statement marked "cancel." If I don't cancel, I will receive 4 brand-new novels every month and be billed just $6.24 per book in the U.S. or $6.74 per book in Canada. That's a savings of at least 22% off the cover price. It's quite a bargain! Shipping and handling is just 50¢ per book in the U.S. and 75¢ per book in Canada.* I understand that accepting the 2 free books and gifts places me under no obligation to buy anything. I can always return a shipment and cancel at any time. Even if I never buy another book, the two free books and gifts are mine to keep forever.

194/394 MDN F4XY

Name	(PLEASE PRINT)	
Address		Apt. #
City	State/Prov.	Zip/Postal Code

Signature (if under 18, a parent or guardian must sign)

Mail to the Harlequin® Reader Service:
IN U.S.A.: P.O. Box 1867, Buffalo, NY 14240-1867
IN CANADA: P.O. Box 609, Fort Erie, Ontario L2A 5X3

Want to try two free books from another line?
Call 1-800-873-8635 or visit www.ReaderService.com.

* Terms and prices subject to change without notice. Prices do not include applicable taxes. Sales tax applicable in N.Y. Canadian residents will be charged applicable taxes. Offer not valid in Quebec. This offer is limited to one order per household. Not valid for current subscribers to the Romance Collection or the Romance/Suspense Collection. All orders subject to credit approval. Credit or debit balances in a customer's account(s) may be offset by any other outstanding balance owed by or to the customer. Please allow 4 to 6 weeks for delivery. Offer available while quantities last.

Your Privacy—The Harlequin® Reader Service is committed to protecting your privacy. Our Privacy Policy is available online at www.ReaderService.com or upon request from the Harlequin Reader Service.

We make a portion of our mailing list available to reputable third parties that offer products we believe may interest you. If you prefer that we not exchange your name with third parties, or if you wish to clarify or modify your communication preferences, please visit us at www.ReaderService.com/consumerchoice or write to us at Harlequin Reader Service Preference Service, P.O. Box 9062, Buffalo, NY 14269. Include your complete name and address.

ROM13R

Stay in the festive spirit next month with Rebecca Winters's
MARRY ME UNDER THE MISTLETOE, the second story
in the sparkling GINGERBREAD GIRLS trilogy!

THEIR HANDS BRUSHED, and the contact sent a warm sensation through her body. His eyes held hers for a moment before he examined the nutcracker.

"I—I love this one." Her voice faltered in reaction to his nearness. "This white uniform makes him stand out. It's an exact replica of the uniforms they wore, down to the black hat and green-and-gold trim on the cuffs and bottom of the jacket."

His husky tone set her pulse racing. "I'll take it."

"Good. I'll find the box for it in the back and wrap it for you."

She couldn't breathe until she was away from him. Good grief. She'd always heard about widow's hormones, but had never given it any thought until now.

Andrea's hands were unsteady as she wrapped the gift in green foil with a red ribbon. He gave her his credit card. She put the receipt in the sack before handing him everything.

"Mom and I appreciate your business." She flashed him a smile. "Merry Christmas. Since I'm closing up, I'll walk you to the door."

Andrea knew she was being obvious, but she wanted him to leave and never come back. It was the exact opposite of her experience with him the first time he'd come in the shop. She couldn't afford to make more of a fool of herself than she already had. He could have no idea that seeing him again had been very hard on her.

Oddly enough, she sensed he wasn't ready to go yet. If he knew she was a widow, he wouldn't be able to leave fast enough, but he hadn't asked.

A tiny nerve pulsed at the side of his hard mouth before he opened the door. "Thank you again for your generosity to my daughter. Merry Christmas." He hesitated for a moment, then left.

To her chagrin, Andrea was strongly attracted to him. His sensual appeal reached down to the deepest part of her, bringing her alive again after more than a year. She was so vulnerable right now, it was frightening. If he came near her again, intuition told her a man like him could become an addiction.

Don't miss
MARRY ME UNDER THE MISTLETOE,
available November 2013—and look out for
Casey's story, the third and final installment from the
GINGERBREAD GIRLS, in December!